Footprints in the Ferns

Lovely Lethal Gardens 6

DALE MAYER

Books in This Series:

FOOTPRINTS IN THE FERNS: LOVELY LETHAL GARDENS,
BOOK 6
Dale Mayer
Valley Publishing

ISBN-13: 978-1-773361-63-5
Print Edition

About This Book

A new cozy mystery series from USA Today best-selling author Dale Mayer. Follow gardener and amateur sleuth Doreen Montgomery—and her amusing and mostly lovable cat, dog, and parrot—as they catch murderers and solve crimes in lovely Kelowna, British Columbia.

Riches to rags. ... Controlling to chaos. ... But murder ... not this time!

One night 10 years ago, 8-year-old Crystal, vanished from her bed in her parents' house, the only clue a footprint in the flowerbed below the girl's window.

Now that footprint's reappeared, this time at the scene of another crime, and Doreen is under strict orders not to stick her nose into Corporal Mack Moreau's new investigation.

But while Mack is busy with the new case, Doreen figures it can't hurt if she just takes a quick look at the old one. Her house is empty, her antiques removed, and she has time on her hands. She's finished working on Penny's garden and needs a new project to keep her busy – and allow her to avoid the heavy work waiting in her own garden. And with the help of her assistants, Thaddeus the parrot, Goliath the Maine Coon, and Mugs the Basset, soon Doreen is busy navigating the world of pawn shops and blackmail as she looks for clues as to what happened to the girl stolen from her bedroom so many years ago.

Surely, it's not her fault when her case butts up against the new one – is it?

Sign up to be notified of all Dale's releases here!
http://smarturl.it/dmnewsletter

Chapter 1

Saturday Early Afternoon ... the same day she closed her last case

DOREEN STAYED AT the hospital for several hours. Penny's surprise attack with a prybar had done more damage than she'd thought. But she was safely behind bars now and wouldn't have a second chance at Doreen and her pets. Mack would see to that.

By the time she was released, she saw Mack walking up the front entranceway to the ER. Her heart lightened as his grin shone in her direction. "Did they call you to tell you that I was done?" she asked as his fingers gently pushed back her hair to check out her stitches.

He nodded, his gaze on her head. "I did ask them to tell me."

"I'm feeling much better. Hopefully Scott will be there when I get home." She didn't want to miss out on his visit. It was too important. On the other hand she was tired and would love a nap before Scott arrived.

"I'm sorry I was detained. I had planned to be here earlier, but, while I was at the office dealing with Penny, something else popped up. We have another case that just came in with footprints, very strange footprints, giving us a connection to a case from ten years ago."

"Oh, interesting." Doreen perked up.

He shook his head. "No, no, no, it's not a cold case. This is an ongoing one and not for you."

"But it is ten years old," she said. "So it's a cold case."

"Nope. Not now it isn't," he said. "It's got nothing to do with you."

She rolled her eyes and said, "Fine, I could use a break. I don't plan on solving footprints in the ferns."

He froze. "Have you heard of the case?"

She tossed a look at him. "What case?"

"A young girl was kidnapped from her bedroom," he said. "And all they left were footprints. Footprints in the ferns outside the house."

Her jaw dropped. "Seriously?"

"Seriously," he said.

She chuckled and then reached up to her head and moaned. "How about you tell me more later. But not now."

Chapter 2

Saturday Afternoon …

BY THE TIME Doreen woke up from her nap, her animals were curled all around her, as if understanding how badly hurt she was. Tired as well, she'd be happy to have a few days with no cold case to contemplate. Sure, getting hurt was her own fault, and she'd be the first to admit it, but, when things came to a crunch, they seemed to always come to a crunch on her.

Mack was right. She kept getting hurt. She had to figure out how to close these cold cases without the same ending. The trouble was, when she talked about putting people away for life, not one of the suspects wanted to walk that path happily. They all tried at the very end to grab that last hope for a bit of freedom. She understood it in theory, but it sucked in real life.

Groaning, she rolled over, spent the next few minutes cuddling the animals, telling them how much she loved them and loved having them in her life. Then her gaze caught sight of the time. It was afternoon already, and, as far as she knew, it was still Saturday, which meant Scott should have been here already or would be at any moment. She took a deep breath and slowly sat up. The room spun a little, but it wasn't too bad. At least her head didn't boom.

She walked into the bathroom and cried out in surprise at her face. She had blood along her temple and something on her cheek, which she scrubbed at. It looked like some medication or maybe iodine. She filled the sink with warm water and, using a washcloth, gently cleaned her hair and face as much as she could.

Somewhat presentable, if she ignored the couple stitches sticking out of her scalp, she changed her shirt to something that didn't go over her head and hopefully wouldn't get more blood on it. Her jeans were bloodstained too. She stripped out of those and put on leggings. Barefoot, she padded downstairs gingerly, then through the kitchen to the laundry room, and loaded up the washing machine, removing any sign of her rough morning.

Her animals had followed quietly behind her. "What's up, guys?" When none answered, she asked again, "Why are you all so quiet?" With an instinctive shake of her head, Doreen felt instant pain because she knew they understood she was injured. She smiled, slowly bending down to pet them all. "I'll be okay. Not to worry. Besides, I'm not so bad I can't feed you guys."

After giving them food, and moving carefully, she wandered the first floor. She didn't remember Mack leaving but presumed he had as the alarms were set on the doors again. She pulled out her phone and sent him a text, thanking him.

Instead of texting her, he called her. "How are you feeling?" he asked.

"Better," she said. "I'm up. I'm downstairs, and I'll put on a pot of tea."

"What, no coffee?" he asked humorously.

"Nope, not today. My head is aching already. Don't think coffee would improve that."

"I don't think the headache and caffeine have anything to do with each other," he said. "This has more to do with the pry bar you left on the workbench."

"Is that what she hit me with?" she whispered, aghast. "I knew I should have found a storage place for that damn thing."

"Are you okay to keep all the tools now, after what happened?"

"Absolutely," she said. "It wasn't the tools' fault. Besides, I'll use them eventually."

He chuckled. "I guess if I need something, I know who to borrow from."

"Anytime. I don't even know what half of them are called."

"I know," he said. "The irony wasn't lost on me."

"But to think she used one of my own tools …"

"She probably thought it was still hers. And George, up in heaven, was probably rooting her on."

"I wonder," she said. "From his journal entries, it seemed like he was saddened by everything that came to pass."

"I imagine he was. You've been asleep for a couple hours, so don't freak out when you look outside and see cop cars."

"Why are cop cars here?" she asked in an ominous tone of voice.

"Because they have to go through the garage, looking for forensic evidence. There's your blood and the attempted murder weapon, etcetera."

She groaned and asked, "How long before the media

finds out?"

"Hopefully not until after Scott leaves. Any word from him?"

As a beep sounded, she glanced at her phone to see a text came in. "I think he's texting me now. I'll call you back."

She checked the text, and, sure enough, it was Scott, apologizing for being late. "You guys stay inside while the cops are here, okay? I'll be back soon." She walked out to the garage and asked the one officer she knew, "Arnold, how much longer will you guys be here?"

Arnold just waved at her and said, "We're almost done. Why?"

"Because I have an antiques dealer coming to look at this stuff." She pointed around the garage. "I need him to have access."

"Not a problem," Arnold said. "How are you feeling?"

"Like somebody hit me over the head with a pry bar," she said with a wince. "And, by the way, where is that?"

"It's in evidence."

She sighed. "I don't really need it for anything, so whatever." She caught the grin that flashed on his face, but he immediately schooled his features into looking sorry for her. She smiled at him. "I know," she said. "I'm not badly hurt. Besides, it's worth it. An awful lot of people will get some closure now."

"We didn't even know we needed to find closure for some of these deaths," Arnold said with half a snort. "What the hell did we do without your help before?"

She thought she heard a really heavy note of sarcasm in there, but she hoped he didn't mean it because she wasn't feeling well enough to deal with it. "Just so long as you realize I'm not doing this on purpose."

At that, he burst out laughing.

She glared at him, her hands on her hips. "I don't deliberately walk into dangerous situations, you know."

"But you do," Arnold said. "And you keep doing it time and time again. On the other hand, the community thanks you. Not one of us would have thought Penny had ever committed murder or even attempted a murder."

"What about George?"

Arnold shook his head. "He was the biggest teddy bear anybody ever knew."

"Which is, of course, why he did what he did," she said gently. "He was trying to protect Penny."

"But the nurse?"

"Once you go down that path," Doreen said, "I guess every other murder gets easier. And, in this case, once again, George was trying to protect Penny. Because the nurse would likely have blackmailed George or confessed and created all kinds of problems."

"So then why didn't George go after Hornby?" Arnold asked. "Just so many unanswered questions."

"George didn't go after Hornby because, I think, by then, George was completely racked with guilt. He knew he was dying, and he wanted to make good so he could go to heaven," she said quietly. "And knowing he had done so many wrongs, he spent the rest of his life trying to do some rights. And, when trying to save Penny, in his mind, then death was justified, but he didn't have any reason to kill off Hornby."

"And yet, Penny had no problem with it?"

"Well, she blamed Hornby for George's death," she said. "After Hornby had blackmailed George, he got serious about committing suicide."

"Any idea what he used?"

"A lot of plants are in their garden," she said, "many of them lethal."

Arnold stopped, peering around the garage into her backyard garden, and she nodded. "I have a lot of lethal things growing in my garden too. But so do you, and you don't even know it." She chuckled at the look on his face. She waved her arm at the furniture. "I just need to make sure the appraiser can take a look at all this."

Arnold stepped closer, looking at the contents with a confused expression on his face, and she shook her head. "You know as much as I do. For all I know, none of this is worth anything, and it's just great-looking junk. But, until I know, I don't want anything damaged."

Thankfully the officers were already packing up their equipment and loading their vehicles. She smiled and waved as they took off, muttering, "I don't have a death wish, you know?"

They hadn't been gone more than a couple minutes as she stood, her face tilted up into the sunshine, before Scott drove up in a rental vehicle. He hopped out and said, "Now that's what I like to see, somebody doing nothing but enjoying the day."

She didn't dare tell him what her morning had been like. "Nice to see you again."

"I hope it's for all the right reasons," he said, rubbing his hands together.

"I don't know," she said. "We emptied the garage of junk and hauled that away, and then we moved up as much as we could from the basement into the garage, but the basement is still full too."

Scott stepped forward, his gaze going to the set of coffee

tables and two pot chairs. His eyebrows rose, and he said, "Well, this isn't quite the same quality or value as the set we already took, but this set will fetch a very nice penny."

She winced. "Could you be a little more specific?"

He chuckled. "I have to go over all the pieces to be sure …" He walked around, counting. "This is, what? One, two, three, four, five pieces here. Four, five, *six* pieces," he corrected himself. "Maybe forty thousand at the end of the day?"

She just stared at him.

He said, "I know that's not as much as you would have liked …"

"It's a lot more than I had thought to get," she corrected. "So selling this set is an absolute yes."

He nodded. "Good." He took some photos and made some notes. "What else have you got?" He wandered around. "This dining room table is easily seventeen thousand. The fact that you have six chairs with original covers on them," he said, "yeah, absolutely. Do you want to sell it?"

"Let me tell you right now that if you want anything here, you can have it if you can sell it for a decent price," she said. "I know some very high-end furniture would easily cost seventeen thousand, but I'm not living at that level anymore. So, if you can get seventeen for this set, please do it."

"Oh, that's what you'll get. We can probably sell it for twenty-three or twenty-four. Maybe higher."

And, at that, she just wandered behind him as he went through piece by piece by piece. He turned, looked at her with a happy smile, and said, "Well over one hundred thousand dollars' worth is sitting here in this garage."

"How much?" she whispered.

He repeated, "One hundred thousand. It depends on

what we can do. These are cherry, specially made, and that maker's mark says they were done for a special occasion. I'll find out how and why and for whom, but just the fact that you have all the chairs in the set ... The set almost always had six or eight. You've got six."

"I can't guarantee there aren't more in the house or in the basement," she said.

"Good."

After that, she wandered around in a daze as he finished up in the garage. Before going to the basement, she took him inside to the living room and the dining room, where she'd stacked up more furniture.

He pointed out the two chairs that went with the set. "Perfect. We'll take those two as well." He looked at the others, shrugged, and said, "I really don't know what these are, or these, unless we can find a few more pieces of it in your basement maybe."

He took some photos, and, just as she led him to the basement through the double doors connecting the two rooms, she got a beep that another text had arrived. She looked at it. *Mack.* She called him and said, "Hey, Scott's here. We're going through the stuff in the garage and the house, about to take him into the basement."

"Does it look good?"

"No," she said, "it looks freaking fantastic. And I still want to know more about the footprints."

He groaned.

"You know what? I'll just go to the library and waste hours and hours looking this stuff up."

"I'll give you what was released to the press," he said, "but that's it. The child was never found."

"Really? No body?"

"None."

"Send what you can to me," she said, "and I'll give you any further details from here, but I've got to go." She hung up on him, and, with Scott's quizzical face, she smiled and said, "Just a case I'm helping the police out on."

She led the way down the stairs to the basement where the rest of the furniture was stored. Scott stopped halfway down and exclaimed in amazement. She pointed to the far back corner where the tallboy was. "I can't guarantee it's what you're looking for," she said cautiously, "but I'm hoping it's the missing piece from the set you took out of here."

He beelined for it and stood several feet away, studying it for a long moment. Then he turned happily and looked at her and said, "You remember how we checked?"

"I wondered if it might have secret drawers," she admitted. "But I didn't want to try to open them and break something."

Now that they were standing right in front of it, he reached around it. "I looked it up, and this one is right here." He pushed something on the far back, and, instead of a small drawer, a long and skinny drawer opened from the side.

She cried out as he lifted up a long strand of pearls. She held out her hand for them and stared in amazement. "These are real, aren't they?"

"That, my dear, is not my field," he said, "but they sure look good to me." He grabbed something from the drawer. "And here is a small note too."

Of course it was in the same feminine handwriting— presumably her great-great-grandmother's. It was a note about how she got the pearls as a gift from her husband on the birth of their first son.

Doreen smiled and said, "I'm so grateful you found these drawers. I haven't even had a chance to see what's in the big drawers. We worked all yesterday and this morning to get access to the pieces down here."

Scott looked around and nodded. "I can't believe your grandmother had so much furniture stored away."

"Neither can I." Doreen motioned at the dresser and asked, "Is there a second drawer?"

"There definitely is." He popped open a similar drawer along the other side.

Doreen smiled when he pulled out a long velvet bag. She held out her hand, amazed to see the dark green velvet. She opened up the end and carefully emptied the contents into her hands. A long jeweled necklace. She whispered, "It can't be real. Surely these jewels can't be real."

Scott lifted the strand of green stones and said, "This is a gorgeous emerald necklace."

She looked down at the rest still in her hand. A matching bracelet and two earrings. She wanted to cry for joy for that connection to her ancestors—more pieces of her family's history. There was also a crumpled piece of paper. She held it up and read it. "For the birth of our first daughter."

He smiled and said, "You don't see gifts like that anymore. Now a wife is likely to get flowers for the birth of a child but certainly not gems like this."

Doreen smiled, gently placed everything in the velvet bag and wasn't sure she could sell any of these. These were part of her family's history, an emotional and happy memory from her family.

Something now very dear to her heart.

Chapter 3

Saturday Late Afternoon ...

B Y THE TIME Scott left, Doreen's head was really pounding, partly from the earlier attack but also with the good news from Scott. Her mind was completely awestruck. Scott would come back later with more answers about his notes. He'd gone away to do some research but had called dibs on several sets of furniture. He was curious about a couple odd chairs. In his words, he'd said, "At this point, I respect your grandmother's acuity in regard to antiques, so I have no idea why she has a few of these pieces here."

"Well, I could ask her," she said.

Scott looked at her and said, "I know it's an imposition, my dear, but is there any chance I could talk to her?"

Doreen's eyebrows shot up. "I don't see why not," she said. "I'd have to call her, of course, and make sure it's convenient."

"Absolutely," he said. "I've taken as many photographs as I want of everything here. And obviously the packers will come back and take that dresser." He looked at it and smiled. "I can't believe you've got a complete set now." He shook his head. "It just boggles the mind."

"And I still have to empty those drawers too," she said.

"Then, of course, as soon as I can, we'll get the items out of the dining room."

"What about the hutches?" she asked, pointing to the back.

He nodded. "They're on my list to do some further research. Maybe call your grandmother, see if you can set up a time to have a cup of tea or something, so I can talk to her. And I'll bring my tablet. We can ask her about some of the pieces in question."

"Sure," she said, "I can ask her right now, if you like."

Of course Nan hadn't been available. Scott had finally taken his leave, as he said, "I've got work to do. I'm still in town tonight. If she's readily available early evening or tomorrow morning, that all works for me."

As soon as he was gone—petting each of the animals as he passed through the kitchen—she dialed Nan again. And, true to form, Nan answered this time. "Where were you?" Doreen asked in frustration. "The antiques appraiser wanted to come and visit with you."

"Oh, that would be lovely," Nan said. "How are you doing with the rest of that furniture in the house?"

"The couch and matching chairs, even several coffee tables, he said he'd be happy to take. I think three dining room sets as well, and, of course, the tallboy we found. But there are a lot of odd pieces, Nan, and I guess he's curious as to why you have those."

"Well, some were missing pieces from sets I heard about in the antiquity underworld," she said. "And then I brought them home, thinking I had a piece of history connected to something nobody else had because I had the odd piece."

"Uh ..." Doreen shook her head. "But then why didn't

you sell them?"

"I couldn't be bothered," Nan said cheerfully. "I think there are about six pieces that belong to incomplete sets because I have the final piece."

Doreen stared at her phone. "Okay," she said, "if we brought you the photos, could you tell us which ones?"

"Probably," Nan said. "Did you find the paperwork yet?"

"No," Doreen said, looking around her living room. "I thought for sure, once we got rid of the main living room furniture, I'd find it."

"It's definitely in the house. Make sure they don't take anything without you having checked it over," she warned Doreen.

Doreen nodded. "I already found a set of pearls and emeralds. Nan, they're beautiful."

"Oh my, pearls and emeralds? I don't think I remember those."

"They appear to be Great-Great-Grandmother's," Doreen said. "They were in the hidden drawers in the tallboy. It had two secret drawers again, but they were long, skinny drawers and full of jewelry. Absolutely stunning pieces."

"And they'll probably fetch a pretty price too," Nan said.

Doreen nodded, but she wasn't sure she wanted to sell them. "I still have to empty the drawers in the tallboy. What time can Scott come to meet with you? He's gone back to his hotel to do some research on some of the pieces you've got here."

"Good," Nan said briskly. "Because every piece I bought, I bought for a reason."

"I'm hoping you'll remember the reason why," Doreen

said drily. "We have an awful lot of furniture here that he's not too interested in."

"Hogwash," she said. "He should be interested in every one of those pieces. I expect Scott to have his truck full, taking everything away. Then you can start fresh."

"That would be nice," Doreen said, "but I don't think I'll have that option."

"Yes, you will. Just bring him here to talk to me. And, in the meantime, find those papers."

"When do you want Scott there? He said later today or tomorrow morning works for him."

"No time like the present," she said. "Bring him by at six o'clock, if that's okay. If not, how about seven?"

Doreen nodded. "I'll check in with Scott and see which one of those times works for him."

"You do that," Nan said. "And, in the meantime, find that paperwork. That'll help jog my memory." And she hung up.

Doreen groaned. Just because Nan said Doreen should find the paperwork didn't mean it was that easy, but first she had to check the tallboy drawers. With the jewels still in her pocket, she went back downstairs into the basement and carefully opened each and every drawer and found they were all full. She walked back up to the kitchen looking for an empty box, but, of course, there wasn't anything. Snagging a couple large plastic hampers, she carried them downstairs and emptied the drawers into the hampers. She unearthed everything from scarves to blankets to some small boxes. Arranging the contents side by side, she carried both hampers back upstairs and wished she had better light and an opportunity to sit down there and look at the items more carefully.

She carried them right into the kitchen, where she set them on the table. Just as she was about to go through them, Scott called her back. She gave him the options to meet Nan. "How about six o'clock this afternoon?" he asked. "I found out some interesting bits and pieces and forgot to tell you about the china set you've got there too. I'll come by, pick you up, and we can go to Nan's place together."

"Perfect," Doreen said. "I just emptied the tallboy. I'm still looking for the provenance paperwork. Nan wanted to see it too because she thought it would help jog her memory."

"Any idea where it is?" he asked anxiously.

"No," Doreen said, gently brushing her hair off her face, careful to not disturb her new stitches, while looking around the kitchen. "I've gotten rid of a lot of stuff, yet there's still so much here to go through."

"My grandmother was the same," Scott said. "If she could find a bargain, she bought it whether she needed it or not," he said with a chuckle. "At least in your case, your grandmother seems to have had a knack for pricey antiques."

"Sure, I just don't know where I'm supposed to find her proof of all of it."

"Keep looking," he said. "I'll be there in about forty-five minutes."

Knowing she didn't have time to go through all the items she'd pulled from the tallboy, she checked for an envelope of receipts or a folder of paperwork of any kind. But nothing like that was in the hampers.

She headed back downstairs, knowing the hutches had drawers as well. She didn't know if they had any secret drawers, mind you, but those weren't likely if they weren't part of the same set. She started at the top right and went through the drawers one by one and groaned at every one because silver and china were inside but no paperwork.

By the time she'd gotten through everything with drawers she found in the basement, she got more and more frazzled. She looked around, but there was no cupboard, so she could see nothing else downstairs that would hide away Nan's paperwork. She'd forgotten to show Scott this stuff in this side room—the cold room, as Mack had called it—and he probably needed to see this stuff too because who knew if any of it had any value. She took a couple more pictures of the big butter churn and a humongous mixer, but it was a floor model—like used in a commercial bakery maybe? She wasn't sure. Still no paperwork was located. If it had been her, Doreen wouldn't have kept it very far away. It should have been upstairs in the office.

But Nan had no office in this house. Doreen stopped, thought about that, and realized the kitchen served as Nan's office.

She headed back upstairs, her gaze going around the dining room, finding no paperwork there. She went around the living room—nothing there. She checked the front closet, found nothing there, and headed into the kitchen. The downstairs wasn't very big, so, unless the provenance folder was upstairs in her bedroom, it had to be in the kitchen. Her gaze landed on the huge pantry full of shelves and more shelves. While some were built-in, it seemed Nan had added a couple cherry standalone shelving units on the short wall. While some canned goods and pet food were in here, most of the shelves held paper goods, whether loose pages or bound books, like cookbooks.

She'd been in and out of that pantry lots of times because she stored some of Thaddeus's and also Goliath's food there. She pulled open the door and frowned at the shelves stacked full of stuff, and definitely lots of papers were on most of them.

Clearing off the kitchen table, she put her hampers off to one side, knowing their contents could very well be as valuable as anything they'd found so far. She removed all the paperwork from the pantry. She didn't have much time before Scott returned. She had one shelf emptied, when she came upon several brown envelopes. One was income taxes from God-only-knew what year. As she peeked inside she could see several years' worth. She checked the others, and one more was income taxes as well, but they were from twenty years ago. She shook her head, placed them off to one side, and looked at the third envelope.

It opened on the side with a twine thread that wrapped around a button to tie it shut. She opened it and gently removed the papers inside. She pulled up a chair to take a quick look and cried, "Eureka."

It appeared to be full of paperwork and receipts and bills of sale. Knowing she was out of time, she closed it up again, grabbed her shoes and a sweater, fed the animals so they wouldn't go hungry while waiting for her to come home, giving them each a hug and a kiss, then secured her home, and stepped onto the front porch just as Scott drove up. She met him in the driveway, and, as she got into his rental car, he looked at the big envelope folder that she carried and asked, "Is that it?"

"I'm not exactly sure," she said. "I haven't had a chance to take a closer look. I figured, if I could show it to Nan, she might recognize it."

"Good idea. Now, where do I go?" he asked.

She pointed out the directions, and, within six minutes,

they pulled into the parking lot of the retirement home. She led him through the front doors and around to Nan's apartment door. Doreen figured it would be unlocked, and it was, thankfully. She called out and led Scott through to the patio. Nan looked at her in surprise, then at the garden path, and said, "Oh, you didn't walk?"

"No," Doreen said. "Sorry, no animals with me today. I'll bring them and the jewelry another time." She stepped to the side and said, "Nan, this is Scott Rosten from Christie's Auction house."

Nan rose, and, in a smooth motion held out her hand, almost as if he should kiss it.

Scott stepped forward, leaned over her hand gently, and whispered, "Lovely to meet you."

And damn if Nan didn't simper. Doreen just stared at her, seeing a side of her grandmother she rarely caught glimpses of. But it was amazing just how much her grandmother responded to the male attention—and yet, shouldn't be so surprising—and how young and lovely she looked. "Scott is in awe of your antique-finding ability," Doreen said.

Nan just chuckled. "I don't know about that," she said. "I just had fun with it."

"And it shows," he said. "Would you mind if I record our conversation, to help me remember all the details about your pieces that we'll discuss tonight?"

"Of course not. Please do." Nan nodded; a wave of her hand was added too. "A large group of us really enjoyed our antiques. We used to go hunting them. Always taking great pleasure when we found a piece the others had missed."

"Did that happen often?" Doreen asked, confused.

Scott shook his head. "I would imagine not often, but,

with big sets, pieces are often lost, and then sometimes a piece gets separated, and nobody realizes its value, and they toss it."

"In our case," Nan said, "we went to a couple big estates, where sets had been sold and individual pieces had been missed. I believe one estate involved a family dispute where one of the sons got a smaller portion of the inheritance, so, in defiance, he took his portion out by taking a few pieces of every one of the antique sets of furniture in the house. Obviously he didn't need the money, but he was more intent on making sure everybody else didn't get the maximum money either when selling the incomplete sets."

"How did you get ahold of that then?" Scott asked curiously.

"He was a friend of mine," she said. "He was getting rid of stuff once he found out he had cancer. So I bought the whole lot off of him."

"So that's why you've got just a pair of chairs here and there?"

She nodded. "Absolutely. And a couple of those other pieces are very expensive."

Scott frowned, held up his tablet, and asked, "These?"

Nan looked at the photo. "Those aren't as valuable." She flicked through the pictures on Scott's tablet and then stabbed her finger on one of the photographs. "These two came from one of the big sets." She flicked over more pictures and then said, "These two, these two, and these two."

Scott looked at the photos and chuckled. "Well, you're right about four of them," he said. "The other two pair aren't as valuable, but it's not about their antique status."

"I don't think the son cared about value as long as he

made sure he broke up the sets so nobody else could sell them for as much money," Nan said. "Families are interesting critters."

"Now the trick is whether anybody who has those pieces is looking for the missing pieces," Scott said.

She nodded. "I figure an auction house like yours, once you put it out in the catalog of what's coming up for sale, should attract some attention."

"You could be right there," he said, nodding. He pointed to one picture of the hutches in her basement. "This is an interesting piece. Where did you get that?"

She launched into a tale. "I'd been down at the local antiques store, where Fen was fed up with having no money, getting no sales, and living in a town full of people too penny-pinching for what he needed to thrive, to even survive. He had rent to pay," she said, "so I bought it off of him cheap."

"How cheap?"

Nan thought about it for a moment and said, "I'm not exactly sure, but I think about four hundred."

"Of course it's worth about seventeen thousand now. You know that, right?"

Nan laughed. "Poor Fen. He could use the seventeen thousand too."

"I know that feeling," Doreen said, shaking her head. "So, Nan, is everything in the basement valuable?"

"Most of it, yes," Nan said. "It's hard for me to say everything is because, at one point, I was struggling to find room to store stuff." She held out her hand for the tablet Scott had. "Would you mind?"

He handed it over, and she slowly flicked through the pictures, coming up with an interesting story for several of

them. Scott was recording this conversation so he had
something further to document the provenance of all Nan's
finds. There was nothing quite like people's memories.
When Nan ran through all the photos and pulled out three
pieces she said were really just garbage, Scott nodded and
said, "You do know your antiques."

"I know some of them," she said. "Those hutches downstairs contain all that damn silverware because it was
impossible to clean."

"Silver?" Scott asked. He turned to look at Doreen.

She nodded. "After you left, I took a look in the drawers,
and there is a lot of silverware," she said, "everything from
cream and sugar bowls and terrines to soup ladles and
cutlery. Tons and tons of it."

"I know," Nan said. "When my nan was alive, it used to
be fun to buff and polish silver together, but I very quickly
learned that was a complete waste of energy. They just
tarnish all over again."

"I don't think I've ever done it," Doreen admitted.

"You won't want to," Nan said. "If you can sell it, do,
please."

"I'll have to take a look at it, but, pure silver of a decent
age is valuable—particularly if you have some provenance
attached to it?" He looked at Doreen and motioned to the
stack of papers in front of her.

"I do. And the china too," Nan said. "Such delicate stuff.
But I always felt like I was in danger of breaking it, so I
could never really enjoy a cup of tea in it."

"Exactly," Doreen said. "I have broken so many old cups
already."

"I did check," he said, "because I did take pictures of the
china with me. I spoke to Randy, and he got very excited and

said that set of china should come back with me and go in the auction. He did give me some details, but honestly I don't remember. China is not my thing, as I said. But I do have it in an email from him that I'll send to you."

"That would be good because lots of boxes of that are in my dining room now too."

"Three sets," Nan said. "Should be three full sets."

Doreen shook her head. "Then, yes, please. Sell it all. I'll just break them."

"Unless you want to keep a set for your children," Scott said quietly.

Doreen winced. "I don't think I'll be having any of my own," she said quietly. "I'm afraid Nan's family line stops with me."

"Isn't that a shame," Nan said.

Chapter 4

Saturday Early Evening...

DOREEN HELD UP the large envelope she had brought with her. "Nan, do you remember this?"

Nan looked at it and smiled. "You found it," she said.

Doreen handed it over to her. "But what did I find?" she asked.

"A lot of the paperwork is in there. There could be a couple more folders like this somewhere. I don't remember if I finally organized everything into one folder or not." She opened it, flipped through, and brought out some of the paperwork. She smoothed her translucent, bony fingers over the surface and said, "See? This is a letter from my nan on that couch set you took away already." She handed it to Scott. "Here's something on that couch still in the basement." She handed that over too, and then she chuckled. "I paid Fen four hundred and twenty dollars for that hutch. Here's the proof."

Scott eagerly took the pages and smiled. "This is perfect," he said. "This is exactly what I need."

Nan was busily shuffling through the paperwork. "There's so much here," she said but with a happy sigh. "I did have a lot of fun. Doreen, you should have a nice little retirement fund by the time you get this all cashed out."

Doreen stared at the paperwork, then at Nan, and asked calmly, "Are you telling me that you have proof of purchase for every major thing in the house evidenced by one of those pieces of paper?"

Nan looked up at her. "Of course," she said. "I never got rid of anything that was valuable."

"Nothing?"

"Well, unless I could trade it for something better," Nan said. "It might take you a little bit to figure it out, and hopefully this paperwork will make it easier on you, but I never got rid of anything. You'll have to sort through the pieces Scott wants, and then maybe he can help you figure out how to sell the rest of it."

Slowly Scott nodded and said, "Absolutely I can." He held out a hand and asked, "Do you mind if I look?"

Nan handed him the stack of papers, and he flipped through it page by page, setting off sheets on one side and a stack on the other. He picked up the smaller stack and said, "These are definitely pieces we'll take this time around. And, of course, I want the letter from your grandmother and a few other pieces there." Finally he looked at the larger stack. "And I haven't even seen these yet, but, now that I know you bought them, we'll go back and take a look at them in person."

Doreen sat back, her heart full of joy. "This has been a perfect day."

"It has," Nan said. "Okay, so what will you do about that new murder mystery?"

Doreen stared at Nan. Then she shook her head and casually brushed her forefinger to her lips, tapping it to make sure Nan knew to be quiet. She might have mentioned something to Scott earlier, but now wasn't the time for all the details. But Nan was having none of that.

"I heard from the police station," she said cheerfully. "I knew you wouldn't wait long before you found something else to investigate."

"I think your inside man is wrong," Doreen said. "I don't have a line on anything new."

"Well, if you don't, you will soon," Nan said in a commiserating tone. She leaned forward, patted Doreen's hand, and said, "I have faith in you."

At that, Doreen chuckled. She caught Scott's confused glance and just smiled at him and said, "Don't even try to figure it out." And she deliberately launched back into a discussion on the furniture. "Do you want to see the pieces that have been pointed out so we can put them aside for taking later?"

He nodded. "Plus, I have to look into these pieces from the missing sets. Do you have any idea who has the other sets?" he asked Nan.

She nodded and said, "The Cartland brothers. There are four of them. Jimmy was the youngest. I don't know if the others still have the rest of the furniture or not."

"So there were four brothers, each got a set, and Jimmy took two from each of the sets?"

Nan chuckled. "He so did. Naughty boy."

"And, Nan, just because they were potentially a good investment, you grabbed them, correct?"

Nan nodded. "I did. Now the question is whether the rest of the family cares about the pieces or not. For all I know, they've been sold many times over."

"I'll have to check into the records," Scott said. He

looked at Doreen. "I would like to go back and take another look though, if possible. And to consider the china and silverware again."

"Well, let's go now," she said, standing up. She leaned over Nan, gave her a gentle hug and a kiss on the cheek. "I'll call you later tonight or in the morning."

Nan walked them to the door and waved goodbye.

Back in his car, Scott said, "She's quite a character, isn't she?"

"That's a good word for her," Doreen said, laughing. "She's into setting up betting pools for everybody in the retirement home too. Gets her into trouble on a regular basis."

Scott burst out laughing. "You know, at her age, I rather imagine she figures she should do what's fun, and everything else and everyone else can get lost."

"I agree," Doreen said. As they pulled into her driveway, she watched Mugs jumping up—or trying to jump up—to look out the window. Without any furniture in front of the big picture window now, he had a hard time. She hopped out, walked up to the front door, and said, "While we go through the furniture, can I offer you a cup of tea or coffee?"

"I'm not much of a tea drinker," he said, "but I'd love a cup of coffee."

She walked in and turned off the alarms, realizing that, pretty soon, she could probably forget about the alarms, only to realize it was again a Saturday. "When's the earliest you can have the men back to pack up more stuff?" she asked, worrying her bottom lip.

"Monday," he said firmly. "I can't get any of that kind of help on a Sunday. But I'm pretty sure I can line them up for Monday."

"That would be the best for me," she said. "The sooner, the better."

"And for us too," he said. "The first set is being cleaned up and won't go to auction for several months."

That stopped her in her tracks for a moment.

"It takes that long to get the pieces readied, photographed, into the next catalog, and then distributing that catalog to the clients. So the sooner, the better for us to process each acquisition. Especially so that the tallboy can take its rightful place along with the rest of the set."

She carried on slowly. "I guess that makes sense. Everything takes time, doesn't it?"

"Absolutely," he said, looking at her. "I guess you had hoped for the money before then, huh?"

"When you're broke, money never comes in fast enough," she said cheerfully. "But I'll make do. And, if there's hope of getting some decent money in a few months, that would be good." Then she stopped, studying him with a narrowed gaze, and asked, "Or do you not pay for ninety days after the auction either?"

"Thirty days," he said. "We have to give the patrons a little time, and that's usually forty-eight hours to clear their purchases, and then we have to do the banking ourselves."

"So it could be four months before I get any money? Is that what you're saying?" she asked, calculating the money in her bank account, in the bowl upstairs, and in her wallet— the cash Nan had given her. Not to mention her earnings from gardening for Penny and Mack. And then she nodded. "I'll be fine," she said. "If nothing else I can always get more jobs to help me out."

"What kind of work do you do?"

She gave him a droll smile as she set their coffee to brew.

"Lately gardening jobs. Before that, I didn't have to work. I was married to a very wealthy man."

"Nice," he said. "Are you sure you're okay to let go of the antiques then?"

"Very much so. Anything to do with that old lifestyle is best gone from my current life," she said with a cheerful smile. She led the way back into the dining room. "These are all the dishes, the three sets, and your men put them all in the boxes the last time they were here."

He glanced at them, took a couple of photos, and said, "I remember these."

She walked through to the living room and the other odd chairs that had been put out first by her and then by Mack. "And I think these were probably the eight odd pieces Nan was talking about."

He nodded. "The four pairs." He knelt forward, looked for maker's marks, nodded, and muttered to himself as he wrote down notes and took more photographs, and then finally he said, "Let's go take a look downstairs."

She led the way into the basement via the living room, and he headed right for the tallboy. He sighed with joy as he looked at it. "I had to reassure myself again it really was here," he exclaimed as he turned to her with a bright smile. "I still can't believe it."

"I think that's why Nan grabbed those chairs out of each set," she said. "Just because she knew they would complete the sets."

He chuckled. "Smart woman." He ran his hands lovingly down the sides of the dresser. "This definitely has to go back with me on Monday." He looked around the room and sighed. "There's some really nice furniture here. A couple pieces over against the far wall are Shaker-style. Not as much money but they're still very nice pieces. If I could get closer to them, I could probably find out the maker and the year—and maybe do some research and see if it's something I could take to the auction house too." He looked at it and said, "It's not my area, but I have seen them go through Christie's, so I'm pretty sure it wouldn't be a problem. I see one side chair, one small couch, and a coffee table in that set."

She nodded. "It's quite nice, fairly plain."

"It's the Shaker style," he muttered. He tried to upend a single chair, but there was so little room to work with here that he had trouble. He wrote down notes and nodded to himself.

She stood quietly, well accustomed to Scott's system by now. She would in no way cause any interruption and break his concentration. He was assessing the pieces, and he could take every last one of these as far as she was concerned.

By the time he had completed his review of the inventory in the basement, he just shook his head in wonder.

"Now up to the garage."

They walked up the big wide staircase, opened the double doors at the top to the garage, and he again worked on the pieces there. Finally he straightened and nodded. "I'll do some more research, but I'm revising the initial number of pieces. Originally I said I wanted fifteen." He checked his notes. "I can't remember now. I have seventeen here circled. But I'm thinking upward of thirty at this point. And I do want to find out about those eight chairs. If nothing else but for the curiosity of it."

She beamed at him. "If you can take that many pieces out of here, I'd be grateful. At the same time, it will give me a ton of room." She motioned at the basement again. "We didn't look at the silverware though."

His eyebrows shot up, and he hurried back down the stairs and directly to the hutches and opened up the drawers, exclaiming the whole time. "If it's a complete set," he said, "it's worth a lot of money." He counted the pieces, turned to her, and shook his head in wonder. "There are several complete sets here. We'll put those through the auction house too."

She felt almost faint with joy when she heard just how much he was taking. She tried to do a count from the basement and the garage, but it was hard to imagine all the pieces he was taking. "Just remember that, if you want everything, you can have it," she said with a bright smile.

"Let me get the pieces I know I can sell," he said. "I'll do research on the eight chairs upstairs in the house. We'll take the china and the silverware."

"You'll bring a bigger truck this time, right?"

He laughed big guffaws of joy. "Absolutely," he said, "I will, indeed." He looked at his watch and said, "Oh, my, it's already past eight-thirty. I need to head back to my hotel room, get some food, and take a couple hours to look this all up. But I'll be back tomorrow morning with my findings." And, with that, he dashed off.

She slowly closed the garage door, locked it, walked over to the side door, and locked it as much as it would lock. She frowned at that, worrying maybe somebody would come in and steal some of these pieces now, realizing she had another day and a half to wait again on the movers. Scott would be back tomorrow morning. But, in the meantime, she had to keep it all safe—by herself. She headed to the kitchen, walked inside, and locked that door as well. Hungry now, as in very hungry, Doreen had a smile across her face, remembering what awaited her in the fridge. "Leftover spaghetti," she cried out. "Yum."

Chapter 5

Saturday Evening ...

DOREEN GAVE THE animals a couple treats each while her plate warmed up in the microwave. It was so hard to contain her excitement at having so many more large pieces of furniture soon to be moved out. Even though they wouldn't be worth anything like the money the big set was worth, it was still money to her that she hadn't had before. As she thoroughly enjoyed her spaghetti—giving bites to the animals so they would leave her alone with the rest of her food—she sat back and said, "Mack, we have to write down this recipe. This is way too good to not repeat every week."

At the mention of Mack, the animals perked up. Goliath purred as he rubbed against one of Doreen's legs. Mugs's tail wagged fast as Mugs danced around, wiggling his butt with happiness. And Thaddeus squawked, "Mack was here. Mack was here." Doreen chuckled at her special family. "Come on, guys. Let's get comfortable."

Smiling, with her tummy full and happy, she grabbed her laptop, plus a cup of warm tea, and sat on one of the pot chairs in the living room, unable to forget about Mack's mention of the child who went missing ten years ago and how the same footprints had once again showed up recently. Without a name, Doreen added a year to her search online. When she came up with the name Crystal Dunham, she texted it to Mack and asked, **Is this her?**

His response was, **Yes, but forget about it.** Then her phone rang, and his voice was brisk as he repeated his text into her ear.

"Not happening," she said.

"You need to heal."

She stared down at the phone, wondering how he made it sound like a reprimand even as his voice was warm and caring. She said, "I *am* resting. I just finished a wonderful plate of spaghetti. I'm sitting here now with a cup of tea. Plus, I'm going to bed early tonight."

"Good," he said. "Is the appraiser coming back tomorrow?"

"Yes. He has to do some research tonight. The movers are coming Monday to pick up more stuff."

"So that's good then, right?"

"Very good," she said. "At this point, the count of pieces he's taking is over thirty and climbing."

There was a moment's silence while she waited for him to respond, and then he exploded, "Thirty pieces! Are you serious?"

"Yes," she cried out in joy, bouncing up to her feet. "*And* the china and the silverware." She could hear his shocked surprise at the other end. "I know," she said. "I still can't believe it. I'm so excited that my stomach is still rolling around, and my thoughts won't calm down. That's why I'm sitting here with a cup of tea. Or I was sitting here. Now I'm dancing around the living room." And she laughed.

"Wow," he said, "you'll be doing very well for yourself

soon."

"Not too soon." She explained about the timelines.

"I can see that," he said. "They want the stuff to go in a catalog to generate some buzz, and then, of course, there's accounting. Normally in an auction you have to pay right there, but I can see maybe, with some of these bigger items, that cashier's checks might need forty-eight hours to process. And, of course, they have to cut checks to the sellers too."

"Maybe," she said, "but I am looking at potentially four months. If not longer. So much stuff is involved in auctioning these pieces that it might take even longer."

"You've been doing okay so far," he said gently. "Will you be okay for a few more months?"

"I think so," she said. "I have some money. Penny paid me a little bit. You're paying me on a consistent basis."

He said, "I forgot to leave you some today, didn't I?"

"Not really," she said. "You're the one who keeps buying all the groceries."

"Yeah," he said, "I do, but that's okay. I don't intend to take it out of your wages."

She grinned. "That's nice to hear. And, in about two months, I should be getting some money from Wendy too," she said thoughtfully. "I think several hundred dollars is down there for me. So it's mostly the next sixty days I have to get through." And then she remembered the five hundred Nan had given her for renting a Dumpster, only they hadn't had to do that. And then she gasped. "The brothers. I never got paid by the brothers."

"The car parts? I thought they handed you a wad of cash or was it a check? I can't remember?"

She stopped and realized she'd put the money in the kitchen and had forgotten all about it.

"Didn't they? Did it bounce?"

At that, her frown popped out. "So I hate to ask …" she said slowly.

"Ask what?" he said impatiently. "Remember that the only stupid question is the one you didn't bother to ask."

"What's a check, and why would it bounce?" she muttered. She clenched her eyes closed and held the phone away from her head.

It started as a gentle splutter. And very quickly turned into massive guffaws.

Mugs, hearing Mack's voice through the phone, barked and barked, jumping up, his front paws on her knee, barking at Mack.

Goliath jumped onto her lap and stared at the phone too. Thaddeus, not to be outdone, landed on her head. She cried out at his awkward slide, using her hair, before he landed on her shoulder. With her free hand, she petted him, and he quickly settled down. When Mack's laughter on the other end of the phone slowly stopped, she glared at it and snapped, "Are you done?"

"Yes," he said, but then several more chuckles escaped.

"Now that's just mean," she said.

"Oh my," he said. "I wish I were there right now, and I could see your face."

"I'm glad you're not here," she said, "because I don't want to see the tears of laughter running down the side of your face. You're the one who told me that the only stupid question was the one I didn't ask, and I asked, and yet, you laughed at me."

"Oh, you're right. You are so right," he said, still struggling to contain his mirth. "I should have had the brothers transfer it electronically."

"Maybe you should have," she said, deliberately not asking what the heck that meant. Cautiously she asked, "But they did give me cash so thanks for the banking lesson."

"If you ever get a check," he said, his voice sobering into a calm, patient teaching voice again, "you take that piece of paper to your bank and give it to the teller. They will deposit it into your account. They will then contact his bank, and they transfer the money from his bank to your account. It can be several days before you can draw on that money though." There was a long silence. "And if they gave you cash why would you say that they didn't pay you?" he asked in exasperation.

"Because I forgot," she muttered. "I dropped it in the bowl and promptly forgot about it."

"It was like three grand," he cried out. "How could you forget that?"

"Honestly because, at the time, I was just happy to get rid of that stuff and the trash by the driveway," she confessed. "I was thinking I'd scored as I wouldn't have to pay for a Dumpster or for a dump run."

He chuckled again. "The brothers were a huge help, weren't they? Not only did they take the stuff off our hands—the garbage and the pallet full of car parts—but they also helped us set up all of George's stuff inside your garage."

"Right. And that was so exciting, not to mention what happened afterward with Penny, that it's no wonder I forgot about the money." She gave a happy sigh, remembering the huge wad she'd been handed. "And just so I understand. I can't take a check to a store and buy something—right? It's not money?"

"Think of it as a promise of money. If you lose it, you are out of luck," he said suddenly in a warning voice. "So you protect that piece of paper. Then you shouldn't have that kind of cash sitting in your house right now either. Remember all your intruders?"

"Got it," she said. "If I'd thought about it, I would have gone to the bank today."

"I had half expected you to," he said. "I didn't even think about reminding you."

"So back to the rest of those questions," she said. "How can a check bounce?"

"The problem with a check," he explained, "is that, when you take it to the bank, and they contact the person who wrote it—in this case, if the brothers had given you a check—if there is no money in the brothers' account, then, even though you have that check, they don't have to honor it."

Her heart froze. "Seriously? So if I ever accept a check I might not get paid. Why would anyone want to take them then?"

"It does happen, so you don't accept checks from just anyone," he said. "And, of course, we always have a problem with, you know, a scam artist passing bad checks. Meaning, checks they already know ahead of time will bounce, but they use them to buy stuff anyway."

"But that's just mean," she said.

"It is," he said. "So, on Monday, you take that cash right to the bank as soon as it opens."

"Okay I'll do that. So if I had a check, can I get money from it right away?"

"Probably not," he said thoughtfully. "It depends on how much money you have in your account. The bank will tell you how quickly a check will clear though. It could be as long as forty-eight hours before you could draw money on it."

"So, in theory, if I put the check in on Monday," she said, "I can buy groceries on Wednesday."

He sobered at that and said, "I'll drop off the money for the gardening tomorrow morning. I should have brought it over today, but that didn't work out."

"I'm okay because I got the cash," she said, "I'm just talking hypothetical situation here."

"Doesn't matter, I'll get it to you soon."

"So is that the girl who went missing?" Doreen asked suddenly.

And he sighed. "Yes. The kidnapping was featured on a TV show. If you can get a transcript of that, it has most of the public details on the case. Obviously not the parts we are keeping secret to help convict our kidnapper."

"Again no ransom note and no sign of her in all these years?"

"No," he said, "none at all. She was only eight at the time, and she could still be alive. I've read about several pretty horrific cases of girls who were kidnapped many, many years ago and are being found alive."

"I remember seeing some of those news articles," she said softly. "I can't quite imagine what those girls went through. But she'd be, what, eighteen now?"

"Something like that. And, if she isn't too badly brainwashed and not too terrified to do something about it, she might eventually have a chance to get free from her kidnapper."

"Right," she said. "Okay, I'm getting off now. I'm petrified once again that somebody else will come in and steal stuff from me, so I've got the security on, but we didn't have security for the outside garage door where Alan Hornby was hiding and attacked me. Although it's got an inside lock, I can't find a key or anything."

"As long as it has an inside lock, make sure that's set, as well as locking the big garage door, then close and lock the kitchen door, and set the alarm," he said. "You should be fine. Nobody even knows about all the other pieces on the property."

"Good," she said. "Anyway, I'll let you go. I'll start researching Crystal's case." And she hung up.

Chapter 6

Sunday Early Morning ...

THE NEXT MORNING, Doreen woke groggy and tired. After all the excitement—Doreen's head-bashing by Penny and the nerve-racking visit with Scott, Doreen's body was just worn out. She lay here for a long moment, cuddling Mugs, who leaned against her belly, his legs stretched out in front of him. Goliath was curled up on the pillow beside her, and, as soon as she moved, his engine kicked in with a huge guttural roar. She smiled and petted him, looking around for Thaddeus, who was on a cardboard box now. "I'm sorry, Thaddeus. I need to get you a roost up here, don't I?" His claws needed to be wrapped around something in order to sleep properly. He could curl up on her shoulder, but she felt that, on a mattress or something soft, he didn't do as well. He really needed places for his feet to firmly grip, and, now that the four-poster bed had been taken away, that was a problem.

She felt horribly guilty. "You've done so much for me," she said, "and here I haven't done anything for you." The closet door was open, and she could see the hanging closet rod. "Maybe I can figure out how to make you a freestanding rack." Thaddeus gave a mild squawk, shifted his position, and let his head drop again. She got up slowly and headed for a hot shower as memories of all her research from the previous night filtered into her brain.

"Crystal, if you're out there, and if you're alive, I'm coming for you," she said, sending out her intentions to the world at large. "If you're dead, I'm so sorry, but I'm coming after your killer then."

Crystal had been taken from a fairly middle-class-to-affluent neighborhood several miles away. The house was built into a hill, and her bedroom was on the hill's high side, her window accessible to the ground.

And that was where Doreen figured the fault of the parents lay. But, of course, nobody ever expected a child to disappear overnight and to never be seen again. Doreen had found a transcript of the TV show and had printed it off but had yet to read it. She figured she'd do that with her early morning coffee. After a long hot shower to loosen up her sore muscles, taking good care of her sore head and her stitches, she stepped out, dried carefully, finding that just bending to dry her legs and feet had her head pounding. She put on a loose T-shirt and leggings and then padded downstairs with the animals at her heels.

Except for Thaddeus. He was crooked into his favorite place at the corner of her neck and shoulder. Downstairs she went through the ritual of once again putting on coffee, one of the most comforting routines in her world. She smiled at that realization. Then she placed Thaddeus on the table, gave him extra seeds because he was feeling poorly and because he'd had a bad night, and then proceeded to feed the rest of her animals.

She wrote down on a notepad *Purchase something for*

Thaddeus to roost on. She still had the one roost in the living room, and that was fine, but he needed another one upstairs too. It wouldn't hurt to have a few hanging around, maybe even a swing or something he could sit on. She'd have to look at the pet stores, as soon as she got some of this money cleared, to see if she could find something meant for birds like him. She wasn't sure how to attach stuff, but she found the internet to be a wild and wonderful place—along with YouTube videos, something she had never had the time or a chance or opportunity to explore in the past.

As she sat there, she remembered the cash from the car parts. After going to the kitchen and getting it, she counted it, then tucked it into her purse, it was too big a wad for her wallet. As she checked her wallet, and there was the five hundred from Nan. For the second time in many, many months she felt absolutely wealthy. With a comfortable sigh, she sat back and said, "You know what, guys? We haven't done too badly. We haven't done too badly at all."

She poured coffee, made herself a piece of toast, and found the leftover muffins from Nan. With a second cup of coffee, she opened up the back door and sat out on the deck with the transcript pages she'd printed off. She took a pen with her and highlighted the items of interest. Eight-year-old disappeared during the night; nobody heard anything; the window was on the shadowy side, and they had a large fern bed. Footprints were found across the grass but only had slight indentations. And there had been an oddly-shaped footprint in the ferns too. There had been photos online, but she had been too tired to study them last night.

She read through the rest of the transcript to see what happened during the abduction. Parents were home; Crystal was an only child, had lots of friends, appeared to be loved by everybody, and, of course, as always, there were no suspects. Doreen wondered at that, then figured it was probably the standard dribble the police said to the media.

With that read, she walked back inside, grabbed her laptop, came outside again, and brought up the photos, but it was a bright sunny morning, so it was hard to see them.

She went back inside, sat at the kitchen table with her third cup of coffee, and looked at the images. The footprints were small with an odd point at the end. Of course, at first glance, it almost looked like a high-heel mark, only it was bigger than that. She shrugged and moved on. And then went back to it, thinking about something else Mack had said the other night when she came home from the hospital. But she couldn't recall what it was, something about having seen the same footprint again. With nothing else to do, she picked up the phone and called him.

"Good morning," he said. "How are you feeling?"

"Like somebody ran me through one of those an old washing machines, and I came out flat and without energy on the other side."

"I told you," he said sympathetically, "that your head wound is nothing to kid about. You had nothing but more stress in the afternoon."

"But good stress," she said gently. "I just went through the case files of what I have on Crystal's disappearance," she said. "And I remember you mumbling something about how you were excited to find the same footprint."

At first there was silence on the other end of the phone. In an odd tone, he asked, "You remember that, do you?"

"Absolutely I do," she said, "so don't try to tell me that I didn't. It was on the way home from the hospital."

"Yes, we have another case," he said. "It has a *similar*, a *similar*-looking footprint," he added for emphasis. "But that doesn't mean it's the same."

"No," she said, "and that first footprint doesn't reveal very much."

"What do you see when you look at it?"

"I see the spike of a high-heeled shoe," she said, "but obviously it isn't."

Mack paused, then asked, "Why would you say that?"

"Because it's too obvious," she said. "If you're stealing a child, would you wear high heels? That's hardly the best footwear for packing off an eight-year-old. Plus, it was dark, and she had to climb a hill. That's not easy in heels either. But, of course, the police would look at that and think some woman was looking for a child of her own. Also the hole is bigger than a heel spike."

"Interesting," he said thoughtfully. "I mean, obviously we had to consider that it might be a woman. But I don't believe we ended up with that suspicion. But the footprint never made any sense to us."

"Of course not," she said. "And this new case?"

"I can't tell you anything about it," he said, his voice businesslike and official.

She rolled her eyes, knowing it was too bad he couldn't see her, and asked, "If you could see me right now, what do you think I'm doing?"

He laughed. "You're rolling your eyes at me and making a face."

"You know me too well," she said, chuckling. "And why can't you tell me anything about the new case?"

"Because it might be connected."

"Nope, can't be," she said, "otherwise you'd have an Amber Alert out. So, therefore, no missing child."

"How very right you are," he said. "In this case, we found the footprint, and we found some things missing from a child's bedroom. But the child is still there."

"So it's not a missing child, it's missing children's things, and the only evidence you have is the fact that some items are gone and this *similar* footprint?"

"Yes," he said, "and that's all I can tell you."

Chapter 7

Sunday Late Morning…

DOREEN THOUGHT ABOUT it for the rest of the morning while she worked in the guest bedroom upstairs, rearranging some of the furniture so it was easier to sort out what Scott was taking and what he wasn't. She still wasn't sure about the eight chairs and was hoping he would explain more when he came by this morning. She also needed to do some major housecleaning.

By the time she was done vacuuming and dusting, she found she'd missed a call on her phone. She quickly dialed Scott and said, "Sorry, I was cleaning up a bit."

"Not a problem. I was wondering if I could come by again now or whenever it's convenient for you."

"Absolutely," she said, "I'll put on some coffee for you."

"Thank you," he said, surprised. "I should be there in about ten or fifteen minutes."

Knowing she only had a few minutes, and with her thoughts on the cold case rolling through her head, she sat down to her laptop to quickly investigate the child's name and her family. As far as Doreen was concerned, somebody had to know who that little girl was and had to know her very well to know where she slept and to access her room. Of course, the fact that there were similarities to another case was fascinating too because why would somebody steal another child's things ten years later? She wondered at the dates. She sent Mack a text, asking if the day of the week on both cases was the same but in different years. He came back with a surprised, **Yes. How did you know?**

I didn't, but I was wondering, she texted. She made some notes for herself on a new notepad and stuck it in a blank folder. When she got up, she saw Scott pulling in her driveway. She walked out to the front to greet him, and he said, "I should have asked if I could photocopy those papers in Nan's file."

"Oh, my goodness, of course you can," she said. "I can work on that now. Nan doesn't really have much of an office. It's at the back of the kitchen."

Scott walked into the kitchen, where the coffee was just now brewing, and lifted his nose appreciatively. He looked around and groaned. "She does like to collect stuff, doesn't she?"

Doreen nodded as she saw this area of the house for the first time through Scott's eyes. The pantry door was open, exposing the floor-to-ceiling shelves, tons of bins and baskets and stuff filling the space. Next to the pantry was an alcove, and the printer/scanner/copier was there. She pulled open the provenance folder and scanned things through the copier. "Will a PDF work?"

"Yes," he said, "and, if you don't mind sending me everything, I can sort it out on the other end."

"But it might include paperwork on some of the pieces you aren't taking," she said.

"That's fine," he said. "I can sort through that too.

Maybe I'll have a better idea of some of the pieces she bought which I don't recognize." He glanced around and said, "Do you mind if I take another look at the dining room chairs?"

She just waved him toward the dining room. "Take a look at whatever you want." He walked through into the other room while she continued to scan. She should have thought to have done this first thing this morning. Why hadn't she? Irritated at herself, she finally finished the job and saw no sign of Scott. She walked through the dining room and into the living room and then opened the living room door to the basement and went downstairs. He was down toward the end, where the stairs led up to the garage. She called out, "Are you okay?"

"Yes," he said, his voice threaded with excitement. "I missed this piece last night." He looked down at a small night table. "It's small enough that it was half under these pieces, but it's a very valuable piece."

She looked at it, shrugged, and said, "I'll take your word for it."

He chuckled. "So, if you're good, we'll make that thirty-plus pieces."

"I've lost count. I'm happy if you take every piece here," she said boldly. "Seriously, I don't want anything that's worth a lot of money. I'll just worry about it being devalued every time I use it. Or about intruders wanting to steal it."

He said, "It's still really hard to see what's here because it's so jammed in together. I was hoping the paperwork would help me clarify that."

"Did you book the movers for tomorrow morning?"

He nodded almost absentmindedly. "Yes, I did that yesterday, but it would be nice if we could get everything this time around."

"I know. I was thinking that myself. What about the eight chairs in the dining room?" she asked hesitantly.

"I contacted Christie's about them, and they're willing to take two chairs for two sets because several incomplete sets have been sold through the auction house. They figure they might sell the matching pair. I have yet to contact the family members, and Christie's isn't interested in taking the other two pairs of chairs."

She nodded with disappointment. "Well, it's still half taken care of," she said with a wry smile.

"I left a couple messages with the family members about the pieces that belong to their sets." Just then his phone rang, and he looked at it and grinned. "Now that is synchronicity." He answered the call while she stepped back, realizing she hadn't yet taken him into the other half of this room. She wandered up and down the aisles in the cold room, looking at the shelves, looking at the pieces that were so not from this time that they were fascinating.

Finally he came around the corner to her. "They want them, but they don't want to pay much for them," he said apologetically.

"How much are they wanting to pay?" she asked.

"I have to confirm the price with you first, but they were willing to pay two-fifty a chair."

"It's not thousands, but at least I don't have two odd chairs I have to get rid of."

"Exactly," he said. "If you're good with that, why don't we arrange for them to come today or tomorrow to pick them up?"

"Good enough," she said. "What about the other two chairs?"

"Still no answer," he said.

"Are they worth much more than that?"

"Not really," he said. "At this point, the price is what people are willing to pay. We'll still have that problem when we go to auction. You could get a better price for a lot of items, and you could get a much worse one."

"Right," she said, understanding. "But five hundred would be five hundred. And I could have it this week maybe."

"Exactly," he said. "If we could get that for the other pair, you'd have another five hundred, and I'm taking the other four with me."

She nodded, then turned, pointed, and said, "I didn't get a chance to show you the stuff in here. I don't think it's up your alley, but I don't know."

He stepped in, noting how different the smell was. "This must have originally been a root cellar." And then he caught sight of what looked like a butter churn and a huge mixer on the floor, and his gaze turned rapturous. "Wow! Your nan was a smart lady!"

"Why is that?"

"Because these pieces, although nothing like the other antiques she bought, definitely have a lot of value attached to them too." He ran his hand lovingly down the beautiful butter churn with its big handle rising out of the top. He pulled the lid off and looked at the churning paddle on the bottom and said, "This would be more of interest to a very specialized collector. Again not my field. But I'll contact somebody about them. Christie's does occasionally take in pieces like this. I'm surprised Nan doesn't have any artwork." He marveled as he looked at the full shelves.

"I don't know if she does or not," Doreen said. "I haven't looked really well down here. And did we even look at the paintings upstairs?"

"I did," he said, "but nothing of any value is there."

"That's good to know," she said cheerfully. "That means I can get rid of them. Some of them are pretty ugly."

He chuckled. "Again it's not necessarily my field, but I didn't recognize any of the artists. What you need is a local antiques dealer who maybe can sell some of the stuff for you and give you a commission on it."

"Absolutely," she said. "Maybe Fen can do that. I really appreciate your help, Scott."

He stepped back and took several photos and sent them off. "One of my colleagues has a passion for this old kitchenware from the pioneering days. And some of this appears to be from ancient England. Almost medieval times—except it can't really be that old. They didn't have these metals then," he said thoughtfully. He stepped back with a happy sigh and said, "Your house is a gold mine."

"It has been so far," Doreen said. She led the way back upstairs. "If you want to keep working down here, that's fine by me. I'll go up and see if all that scanning came through."

"If you don't mind then, I will stay here," he said, heading back into the furniture section.

Doreen walked back upstairs, her steps light. If she could just empty this house of all its furniture, she'd have so much space. Sure, some pieces weren't worth much, but other pieces were obviously worth a lot. And, for the first time, she found herself thinking of this as her house. In the kitchen alcove, she checked on the scan and found it was all good, quickly sending Scott an email with the PDF attached and then sent herself one with the attachment as a backup. Then she placed all the paperwork back in Nan's folder and put it on the shelving in the kitchen pantry. As she looked at the shelves, she just groaned at the books, the loose papers, and all kinds of other stuff. She'd deal with all that later.

She returned to the alcove, happy that Nan's old printer still worked—that was all Doreen cared about in here. Except for the small hutch the printer sat on though.

She looked at it, frowned, bent down, opened the doors, and found even more paperwork underneath. She groaned and pulled that out. She hadn't even considered that paperwork would be in here when she went looking for Nan's provenance file. She flipped through some of the loose papers, but there wasn't anything of interest. Unless this hutch … When she heard Scott's voice behind her, she called out, "Is this of any value?"

He took one look at the hutch and smiled. "It is," he said. "May I?"

She backed out of the alcove and stepped into the kitchen area. He bent down, checked it out, and said, "I could take this too, if you want."

"I want," she said.

He nodded. "You'll have to unload this hutch before I can take it, and then you'll need something else to hold the printer."

She winced at that. "I can move it to the kitchen table, but that's not ideal either."

"This piece was probably put in here because it fits," he said. "Often that's the only reason things get moved where they are."

"Once you take away all the rest of the furniture," she said, "I'll see what's left, what would work here for the printer."

He chuckled. "There won't be a lot because we're taking

most of it."

"Then you're helping me clean out Nan's junkyard," she teased.

"Her *expensive* junkyard," he corrected with a smile. He turned toward the pantry, looking inside, and said, "An awful lot of papers and books are in this pantry as well."

"I know," she said, groaning. "I have no clue what to do with these books, but they're ancient."

He looked at them, and his jaw dropped.

Chapter 8

Sunday Late Morning ...

AS DOREEN WATCHED, Scott reached out a shaky hand and gingerly chose a book.

"Oh, Nan," he said, and he flipped through the pages gently. "These are probably the most expensive items you have in this house."

Doreen stopped, stared at him and the book he held, and asked, "What's a Totomus?"

"This book is a very expensive original by Totomus, an author from long ago," he said. "But again it's not my field." This time, instead of taking a photo, he called somebody. "John, I have in my hands a first edition 1717 Totomus," and he spelled out the title and the author's name.

There was an explosion of sound on the other end of the phone.

"Yes, I'm at the same house, where the grandmother spent her life buying antiques and stuffing them away for the granddaughter. We just walked into the pantry of the kitchen, and raincoats are hanging on the edge of this bookshelf holding rare books," he said, and then he stopped and stared at the bookshelf and shook his head. "And it's a hell of a bookshelf itself. Looks like old cherry, but I can't even see it for all these books. However, the books are not in any temperature-controlled atmosphere," he said in a faint whisper. "They're just sitting here."

As she watched, he added, "There's also a limited edition *Ulysses*." Then he read off the date.

Doreen realized she hadn't even considered these books might have value. When Scott finally put away his phone, he said, "So this friend of mine is a dealer in specialized books. He said he would like very much to come and take a look. He consults for Christie's, but he also has his own private network of collectors."

"When can he come?" she asked.

"Tomorrow morning. He's taking the red-eye out of Toronto tonight."

"It's really a big deal then, isn't it?"

Scott smiled gently. "My dear, you have no idea how big a deal this is. I don't know how many of these books are valuable, but he wouldn't fly all the way here to see them for nothing."

"Let's hope there is at least one worth money," she said with a happy sigh. "Who would have thought Nan would hide so much money in this little run-down house?"

"Obviously she didn't spend any on upkeep of the house," he said as he looked around and asked, "Is there an attic? Hopefully. I'm just wondering if you have more hidden rooms."

"There is an attic. I have been up in it," she said, "but it was mostly empty. Just a few boxes of old clothing."

"You may want to take a second look," he said. "And I would open every closet, every nook and cranny, and take everything out. That's the only way you'll know, particularly with John and me both here tomorrow."

"Sheet music?" she asked.

His frown was instant. "What do you mean?"

"I just caught sight of it in that hutch underneath the printer," she said slowly. "It was a large folder, and I peeked in, and it looked like sheet music."

He shrugged. "I have no clue. John might. I don't know."

She walked over to the hutch and opened up the double doors underneath. On the bottom, where she had flipped through the paperwork, she pulled out the folder and noted its leather binding. "I think I need to contact Nan again," she said. Slowly she held out the binder.

He looked at her, then looked at the sheet music. "None of this means anything to me," he said, "but John might know."

"Good enough," she said. "I'll visit with Nan again."

"You do that," he said, "and tape the conversation so you don't miss anything."

With that, he took off, promising to return the next morning at nine with another truck. She was so stunned at the recent turn of events that she wasn't even sure what to do. But the fact was, one person had answers to this mess, and that was Nan. She called her grandmother.

"Oh, there you are," Nan said. "I was wondering how you were doing."

"Nan, did you know some of these books in the kitchen pantry might be valuable?"

"Of course they are," Nan said. "I bought a whole pile of valuable stuff, thinking of you."

That just boggled her mind. Some of these would have been purchased when Doreen was just a child. In her mind, she thought Nan had done this because she was afraid Doreen's marriage would break down, leaving Doreen destitute—and she'd been right—but all these items? "Yes, but, Nan, like, this stuff is *really* valuable."

"And that's fine. Although some of it I don't remember where I got it from," she said. "Especially the books. I had some given to me as"—and her voice lowered almost to that girlish tone again—"special gifts. A couple men knew I was collecting pieces and often gave things to me."

Doreen just shook her head as she stared at the stuffed bookshelves. Not even really bookshelves but shelving. She wasn't sure where one piece ended and the next started, they were all so full. "Oh my, how come I didn't even look at this corner?" she wondered out loud. "All this time I was looking for the provenance paperwork, and I never thought to look in here."

"That's because it's mostly recipes and junk, and you would have seen that much already. Besides, that's all boring stuff. I'm sure you'll sell it and make some nice money off it," Nan said as if she didn't have a care. "Tell me more about this case."

"Do you remember a young girl being stolen from her bed at night?" she asked. "Crystal Dunham?"

"Oh my," Nan said in a hushed whisper. "That was very sad."

"What's the gossip on it?"

"I think people thought it was more of a parental abduction. Until she didn't show up again."

At that, Doreen sat down. "You mean, the parents were divorced?"

"Yes," she said. "And it was a fairly recent divorce. I believe it happened at the father's house, and his new girlfriend was living there when Crystal disappeared. I don't remember when they got married. It raised a lot of eyebrows at the time."

"Meaning, he got married right after his daughter was kidnapped, and people didn't understand?"

"Maybe," she said, "or maybe it was the other way around."

"Do you know the stepmother?"

"I don't know that I've ever met her," Nan said drily. "The stepmother was living in the same house when the girl was kidnapped I believe, but you can't quote me on that. I think I heard the parents had separate houses across from each other, and the girl went back and forth. I just don't remember for sure. They only live a mile or so away from here." And she spouted off the street. "I can't remember the number, but it's at the end of the road. A dead end too, I believe."

"Anybody living here now who may have more information on it?" Doreen asked. "Any family relatives?"

"I don't know," Nan said. "I'll have to ask around."

"Do that," Doreen said, adding, "Maybe this time we can solve the case before anybody dies."

Nan chuckled at that. "You do realize the case files from Penny's cold cases are still supposed to be coming to you from the journalist?"

"They will probably help the police as they sort through this mess with Penny."

"I do wish she hadn't attacked you," Nan said crossly. "That's hardly fair. You were only trying to help. And definitely not ladylike. I thought better of her."

"I used to be a lady, and I'm certainly not acting like a lady these days," Doreen said. "And I don't imagine Penny gave a damn at that point as she was thinking about finally having a few years of freedom herself."

"Yes, but to try to hurt you, that's just not acceptable," Nan said.

"Let's go back to the antiques. You need to tell me exactly what is in this house that is valuable," Doreen said abruptly. "Scott and I were struggling as to what could be worth money here."

"I spent fifty years collecting, my dear."

"And yet, you said you collected this all for me, but I'm not even thirty-six yet," she said.

"Sure, but I collected before that, and then I would trade up and move things around. It was a fun hobby. And I figured that, if I ever needed money, I could sell it. The good news is, by the time you came along, I no longer needed money, but you did."

Chapter 9

Sunday Noon ...

DOREEN SUDDENLY HAD an idea. "Nan, what if I picked you up and brought you home so you could walk through the house and tell me exactly what I should be watching out for?"

"Oh, that'd be lovely," Nan said in delight. "Why don't you come and get me now? I can have a cup of tea at your place." With a chuckle, Nan hung up.

Doreen quickly walked out to the car and drove to the retirement home.

Nan already stood outside. She crawled into the front seat of the car and said, "This is exciting as I haven't spent much time at home since you've arrived."

Doreen felt guilty. "I'm so sorry," she said. "I never even thought of that. I should have invited you back more often. You know you can come over anytime, right?"

"I've been there several times," Nan said. "At least I think I have. I think after you got hurt."

"Right." Doreen gave herself a mental shrug. What was she talking about? Nan *had* been here several times. Or was it Doreen who was losing it? She groaned softly.

As Doreen pulled in the driveway, Nan chuckled to see the animals jumping at the window. "You really should get them a big bench or something right there so they can keep an eye out."

They walked into the house, and Nan greeted all three animals. Doreen stood in the doorway and watched the big love fest. She leaned against the door and again felt bad. She should have had Nan back here every second day. What the heck was wrong with her? She walked through, calling back, "I'll put on the teakettle, Nan."

And she did just that. When she turned around, Nan walked through to the kitchen porch and stood outside. "Oh my, it looks so much different without all the fencing back there," Nan cried out in excitement. "It looks huge." She gazed at the creek and smiled. "Why did I never think of that?" she said. "I was always so worried about the water coming in the yard, but, of course, the fence wouldn't have stopped the water from going where it wanted."

"No," Doreen said, "and I arrived early April this year, but this has been a mild springtime, right?" At Nan's nod, Doreen continued, "I know the creek water can get higher at this time, but I'm hoping it'll behave itself for a few years so I can get this backyard done."

Nan said, "The land does slope down here. You might want to put in a low retaining wall close to where that fence used to be so the water will stay on the other side."

Doreen nodded. "That's not a bad idea. I was thinking to make it a grassy slope because, if the water does rise, it won't hurt the grass."

"Or you could do that too," Nan said. "It does give you a really pretty view this way, doesn't it?"

When they walked back inside, Doreen pointed out the

books on the table. "I *think* these are valuable."

Nan looked at them, nodded, and said, "Six first editions." She walked over to the bookshelf and pulled out several books on the top shelf. She stacked them on the kitchen table and said, "These are quite valuable too, but there was a rare one here somewhere." She returned to the pantry, moving slowly along, tapping her finger to her lips, studying the books on the top shelf. "I don't remember so much stuff being here," she said. "How can you possibly find anything?"

Doreen laughed. "Exactly my problem."

Nan shot her a grin and went to the next row. She lifted up a whole pile of papers, looked at what was left, then put down the papers again, and said, "You know what you should do when you empty that living room? Just take everything out of here and put it all in one big pile to sort through."

"You're not the first one to make that suggestion," Doreen said. "I was trying to do that with the closet upstairs."

"That closet is stuffed," Nan said. "At one point, it was a bit of a game to see if I could put anything else in it. But I had a lot of fun with stuff back then. Now I enjoy empty spaces."

Nan next lifted up more paperwork off one shelf, set it back down, and then lifted another stack of what looked to be printed-off pages. "Aha." She set aside the papers and grabbed a small book and handed it over. "It's a special book of poems," she said, "by Byron."

Doreen didn't hear the rest of the name. She gently blew the dust off the book and stacked it on top of the others. "Apparently some book expert is coming tomorrow to take a look at these. Are any of the others worth anything?"

"Those are the big money," Nan said, pointing to the stack on the kitchen table. "But you might as well take them all off the shelves, give them a good dusting, and let him pick and choose. I know another couple are worth a little bit, but I don't think they're worth anything like what these are."

Nan pulled out the rest of the books and stacked them on the nearby kitchen chair. "I'll just leave them here for him to sort. I don't think any more books are in the pantry, but there's everything else still." She turned and scolded Doreen. "This place really is a mess."

Doreen's jaw dropped. "Seriously?" she cried out. "I've only been here barely a month. This is all your mess."

"Oh, I know," Nan said complacently. "The good news is, I don't have to clean it up ..." She gave Doreen a big fat smile, then chuckled. "You do."

Doreen groaned and heard the teakettle whistle. She walked over and made a pot of tea. "What about the sheet music?" she asked Nan. When there was no response, she turned toward Nan and said, "Nan?"

But Nan appeared lost as she looked at her quizzically.

"Earth to Nan," Doreen called out. "Earth to Nan?"

Nan gave her a small head shake. "Music," she said with a smile. "Yes, some of those were original songs, unpublished by some artists. I bought all that stuff in an estate sale, and he was an artist himself."

"An artist?"

"A musician," Nan said with a wave of her hand, as if that lumped everybody who did any creative form of work as an artist. "He was a very interesting chap."

"Do you know if the music has any value?"

"I paid a pretty penny for it," Nan admitted. "At the

time I was sleeping with him, only he was looking for somebody to look after him."

Doreen just blinked at the idea of Nan sleeping with the artist. "So he was looking for a sugar mommy?"

"Yes, something like that. I guess *a patron* is what they would have called it way back when. We were together for about a year," she said. "And then his music took a darker turn. I couldn't stand his moodiness. We broke it off. I'm not even sure where he is now. I think he died of an overdose," she said thoughtfully.

"If we had his name, it would help."

"Not really," Nan said with a shrug. "He never made it big, and the music isn't his. It belonged to another artist. I think three packets of music are around here somewhere. I paid for them at different times, I believe. It should be in that paperwork."

Doreen brought out two more packets of music she had taken from the hutch. At that, Nan studied the hutch and said, "You should probably get your Christie's guy to look at that piece too."

"He already has," she said. "He wants to take it."

"So empty it and move all that stuff off the top. Just make more of a mess." Nan laughed.

"Which is why," Doreen said, "I'd like to go through as much of this as possible before they get here, and then, if they're interested in selling anything, I'll let them have it."

"Of course you will," Nan said. "I don't remember half of the stuff anyway. Lots of it'll be useless. I went through phases where I bought and sold more exotic books, then furniture. At the end, it was all just stuff of value that would make a difference to you and none to me. Is the tea steeped, dear? I suddenly want a warm cup of tea."

Doreen nodded and poured two cups, added milk, and asked, "Do you want to sit here or outside?" At that, she found the chairs in the kitchen were half full of books now. She groaned. "I really do need to get this place cleaned out."

"Of course you do," Nan said. "How about in the living room?" Then she walked into the living room and stopped. "Oh my," she said. "I didn't notice when I first came through, since I was having so much fun with the animals, but this looks amazingly huge now."

"It does, doesn't it?" Doreen said with a chuckle. "These are the eight chairs, of which Scott is taking four, and apparently somebody he spoke to from the Cartland family is taking two of them. I don't know about the other two."

"Then you've done well for yourself," Nan said with a note of pride. "If you even sold half of what's in here, you've done well."

"I think Christie's will end up taking well over forty pieces," Doreen said. "But I would love for Scott to take everything."

"Not everything is likely to be of high value," Nan said. "Christie's will only want the best."

"You don't have any artwork, do you?" Doreen asked, remembering Scott's words.

"Not really. I had some pieces, and I sold some. I think there's one still hanging around in a closet. It was godawful ugly," she said, "of some woman dressed in black in a half sitting position on the edge of a couch." She gave a head shake. "It was terrible."

"Maybe it's terrible, but is it priceless?" Doreen laughed at that.

"Probably," Nan said. "It was ugly enough." At that, Doreen looked at her, and Nan laughed again. "You don't think most of this stuff is nice, do you? I think most of it is ugly."

Doreen shook her head, reached out her arms, and engulfed Nan in a very gentle hug. "I'm so delighted to hear you say that," she said happily. "I was feeling so guilty for selling these pieces, but honestly they're awful."

Nan let out a peal of laughter. "They are," she said, "but, if you pulled these eight chairs from the basement, I presume you also got access through the garage, right?"

"Come see," Doreen said. "You also haven't seen George's workshop that we moved over here." She led Nan through the kitchen door and out to the garage. With the light on, even though it was stuffed full of furniture, it was obvious all the boards and tools were hanging up and the workbenches were all along the walls.

Nan stared in amazement. "Oh, wow, this is lovely. I don't know what you'll use the tools for, mind you, but they're there if you need them."

"Exactly," Doreen said. "And Scott has claimed a bunch of these pieces, although I don't think he is taking all of the furniture."

"He needs to take that set with the couch and the pot chairs," she said.

"Yes, and the three coffee tables that go with it, so that's six, plus the tallboy still downstairs in the basement, and I think the two dining room table sets with the matching chairs," she said, pointing out one dining room table with the chairs upside down on top of it. "I don't know about these pieces here." She motioned to a couple dressers close by.

Nan shook her head. "I don't remember either of them," she said with a shrug. "But that coat rack, it's original." She pointed to a tall piece standing in the back corner. "That's worth a lot of money."

"I don't think he mentioned it, but I can't remember anymore," Doreen said doubtfully.

"You need to point it out. It was in the White House way back when. I don't remember the history now. I think it's on the receipt."

"Maybe," Doreen said with a shrug. "I'll mention it to him at least."

At that, Nan wanted Doreen to open up the double doors to the basement. She opened them, and they walked down the stairs. "This is one of the best ways to get stuff up and down," she said. "It was ingenious."

"Any idea why they had these stairs put in?"

"Nope, but whoever did, like I said, it was a perfect solution. This house is old. It was built like in the 1930s, even the 1920s maybe," Nan said. "I'm not sure what the double doors were used for, but these doors were here when I moved in, and I thought it was pretty amazing to have access to the basement from so many avenues."

Downstairs, Nan looked at the half-cleaned-out room and shook her head. "Still so much stuff is here."

"I know," Doreen said drily. "And I've worked really hard to clean it out."

"Hopefully he'll take most of this." Nan walked over to a hutch and said, "He needs to take this."

"That and the silverware inside." Doreen nodded. "And I think one of the dining room sets down here too. I'm not sure." She looked at the furniture to see more dressers, more chairs, and more dining room tables. "Did you buy all this stuff randomly?"

"I was part of a large group of some really avid antiques

buyers. It got to be more fun to bid against them and just take stuff out from under their noses. At the beginning, I didn't know what was good and what wasn't, but, if someone in the group was bidding on it, then it had to be good," she said. "Of course they burned me a couple times, and I ended up with pieces of junk, but that was pretty fair on their part too. I made them spend more money on some pieces and literally didn't let them get some pieces they really wanted," she said with a small shrug. She turned and said, "Now, how about we go sit outside?" And she made her way back up the stairs.

At the top Doreen closed and locked the doors again and led them back into the kitchen. "Did you think of anybody at the retirement home who might have any connection to Crystal's family?"

"Haven't had a chance yet," Nan said. "I've got to think about some of the Dunham family history, but I can't remember anything about it. I think her mother worked at the hospital though."

"The hospital?"

"Yes," Nan said, "but I don't remember much. Just that she was a nurse. I think a nurse. Maybe she was the dietician at the hospital." She shook her head. "For all I know, she could still be there."

"If she is, I'd love to talk to her," Doreen said. "But, of course, it'll be painful to bring up that case."

"Not as painful if you solve it," Nan said with a crafty tone of voice. "That's what's needed. Her whole life's been put on hold, waiting to find out news about her daughter."

"That would be heartbreaking," Doreen said. "I can't imagine."

"Exactly," Nan said. "Her name is Clara," she cried out

triumphantly as she pulled the name from her head. "And I don't think she ever remarried. So you should find her on the staff list at the hospital."

"I'll take a look." Doreen wrote the name down on her notes.

Nan finished her cup of tea and said, "You don't have anything to go with our tea, do you?"

"Not really," Doreen said. "We could go out for lunch."

"That would be lovely." Nan looked at her in delight. "Why don't we go to the Chinese food place? I haven't had their buffet in years."

Chapter 10

Sunday Lunch ...

ON THAT NOTE, Doreen grabbed her purse, intent on
paying for lunch. She locked up the animals, grateful
for a chance to get out of the house as she drove to the
restaurant. After they were seated, she got a text from Mack.
She told him where she was and then walked around the
buffet with Nan, filling her plate with food. She hadn't
realized what a huge selection of food was here and how
cheap it was. Even if she just had one meal a day here, she'd
never starve again. Then she mentally calculated what that
price would look like on a monthly basis and winced. Maybe
it was still cheaper to learn to cook. But she would get her
money's worth today or die trying. When she sat back down,
Nan was eating almost as much food as Doreen was.

Concerned, she leaned forward. "Nan, do you get
enough food at home?" she asked in a low voice.

Nan looked at her in surprise and nodded. "We get lots
of food, dear. I love hearing that you're worried about me."

"I don't like being worried about you," Doreen admitted. "I'm afraid you're always giving me money that you
need for yourself."

"Nonsense," she said. "I was just thinking about how sad it would be to lose a daughter, like Clara did." And that firmly brought the conversation back to the cold case.

"There has to be a reason why Crystal was singled out. One article I read was about a man who'd been doing odd jobs for a family and who had stolen the girl from her bedroom. She was found a good many years later, but, of course, that's not the same thing as what's happened here."

"No, but it doesn't mean it isn't similar," Nan said thoughtfully. "I'd love to think that little Crystal is alive."

"I know," Doreen said. "Yet it's got to have been pretty rough on her if she was somebody's captive for such a long time."

"And yet, in some ways, maybe not," Nan said. She took several more bites. "Crystal and Clara didn't look alike," she said abruptly.

Doreen, in the act of taking a bite of her chicken wing, slowly lowered it as she chewed. "What do you mean?"

"They just didn't. I can't remember the details now though." She frowned, stared at her plate and then off into the distance.

Doreen rushed to make her feel better. "It doesn't matter that you can't remember every detail," she said. "It was ten years ago. Because she was young and often kids don't look like one parent or the other."

"Sure it was," Nan said, but she didn't look terribly convinced. "But you can probably get an image of Crystal online."

"I have seen a picture of her," Doreen admitted. "But I haven't pulled one up of her mother."

"It's a pretty small town. And, after the kidnapping, Clara didn't want to move away because she was afraid her daughter would come home looking for her, and she wanted to be here."

That pulled at Doreen's heartstrings in a big way. "I can see that," she said, "but it still breaks my heart to hear it."

"I know," Nan said. "It's just brutal, isn't it?"

"Yes," Doreen said. "Even hearing about people losing their pets makes me feel terrible. If somebody stole Mugs, I don't know what I would do."

"Right, same for Goliath and Thaddeus," Nan said. "I wish they would let us bring pets into a restaurant like this."

"I know," Doreen said. "I miss them. When I'm gone too long, I find I have to run home so I can cuddle them."

"That's the way it's supposed to be," Nan said stoutly.

By the time they were done with lunch, and Doreen had Nan back to her Rosemoor apartment, Doreen was more than grateful to head home herself.

As soon as she got in, she sat down in one of the pot chairs and spent time cuddling all three of her animals. Even Mugs made it onto her lap, and Goliath was half lying on top of her with Thaddeus wrapped up in her neck. She stayed like that for over half an hour, just loving that she had a family. Sure, a fur and feathered-bodied family, but they loved her, and she loved them.

At this very moment, she was damn grateful to have them in her life. She stroked them carefully and gently, holding still as long as she could, but then finally the combined weight of the large Maine coon cat and her dog was too much. She pushed Mugs off gently so he went down, and then Goliath jumped off.

Without realizing it, she dozed off. When she woke up again, she shared the chair with all three animals once more. She had to laugh at that. It was already well after three, and, although still tired, she felt better. The events of the last few weeks, especially Penny's attack, had caught up with Doreen. She needed a good night's sleep, but maybe fresh air would help for now.

She straightened up, walked into the kitchen to find treats for each of the animals, and then said, "How about we go for a walk?" They all jumped up and down, and Mugs did something she'd never heard before—he opened his mouth and howled. Back at her laptop she checked how far away Clara's house was, using Google Images to pick out the correct one—if Nan was right. Doreen guessed it looked to be a good two miles from here, so it would be a four-mile walk round trip. She winced at that but filled a bottle of water and said, "Come on, guys. Let's go!" And they went out the front door this time and back toward town.

"It's really nice out here today," she said to Mugs. He barked a couple times. She followed the creekside path, everybody more than excited to be out and about. "We haven't done enough of this. At least not walks to explore." She laughed at Goliath racing ahead and rolling around on the path while waiting for the others to catch up.

Lately their walks had led to Penny's house. Doreen had no clue what would happen to Penny's house now that Penny was in jail. Although if she was released on bail she needed a place to live. And could still sell it from inside the jail if she didn't get out any time soon. And Doreen certainly had no desire to keep walking in that direction.

Instead, she walked toward where more Chinese food was—not the buffet restaurant but her takeout place—and, as they walked past it, Mr. Fong Wu was there. He waved a hand, and she waved back and smiled. A hairdresser was next door. Doreen didn't know the lady's name because Doreen had yet to take the time to look after her own hair, but everybody held up a hand and greeted her as she went by. In her old hometown that would never have happened. Everybody would have looked the other way so you *wouldn't* make eye contact. But here, everybody was so friendly.

By the time she walked past what she figured was the two-mile mark and came up to the street where Clara was living, Doreen found a ravine and some hilly ground.

As she came up to the house where the kidnapping had occurred, she saw the front of the house was on high ground and it dropped down in the back of the ravine a little bit, so it must have a walkout basement that led to the pool against a retaining wall. So this was Crystal's home.

And Clara was currently living across the street. Doreen wondered about that. She understood the reasoning to be close to her daughter but to live across the street from her ex? No way. Doreen walked along the block itself, and it came to a dead end. She walked back down on Clara's side, studying her house and its proximity to where Crystal's dad lived too. "If I ever divorce with kids caught in the middle," she said, "I'm not sure I'd want to stay on the same block. I guess it would depend on the relationship with my ex."

As she walked past, she had to step out of the way of a small red car that pulled up and parked in the driveway. Doreen walked past as the car door slammed shut.

Then a woman called out, "Are you Doreen?"

Doreen turned, surprised, but she nodded. "I am."

The woman smiled, motioned at all the pets around Doreen, and said, "Those really are a dead giveaway, you know?"

"I guess they are," Doreen said. "But they're family, so I don't even think about it."

"What are you doing in this neighborhood?" the lady asked curiously.

"I was looking for other places to walk," she said. "The animals and I like to explore a lot."

"Do you live around here?" the woman asked. "I don't remember seeing you here before."

Doreen decided that good manners only went so far, and she said, "No, not really. I live a few miles away. I didn't catch your name, by the way."

The woman looked momentarily embarrassed and said, "Sorry, I'm Clara. I'm Clara Dunham."

"Oh, hi," Doreen said. She glanced across the road and back at Clara and frowned.

Clara nodded. "I see you've heard about my case."

"I'm sorry," Doreen said, nodding. "Losing a child has to be completely heartbreaking."

"It's the worst," Clara said simply. "It's seriously the worst."

There was an awkward moment when neither had anything else to say; then Doreen turned and said, "It was nice meeting you," and kept on walking. She turned back once, and the woman was no longer outside but had gone into her house. Still, it was puzzling. Who could possibly know Crystal well enough to know where she slept? Surely that limited the suspect pool to friends of the family, workmen, other children's parents ... As Doreen thought about that and the friendliness of her new hometown, she found that meant the suspect pool was a very big ocean indeed.

Chapter 11

Sunday After Noon ...

ON HER RETURN trip home, Doreen thought about Clara's case and finally concluded there were so many possibilities as to suspects that the number had to be narrowed down. She thought about going back and asking Clara about it and decided against it. Doreen slowly walked home, studying the avenues, studying the roads. This was a dead-end lane, so somebody who drove down here would have to turn around and come back out again, which would increase their chances of being seen. Not very smart for a kidnapper.

Now Crystal did live at the last house on the block, so somebody could have just carried her right down into the ravine and out to the next street and to a vehicle. She wondered how many people would think of going that way. She herself would because it would give her more cover. Which kind of said her mind was going off in the wrong direction these days.

As she went to cross the road, she stopped and stared back up at the house where Crystal had disappeared from, to see Clara coming toward her. This time she had on a vest and her running shoes. Doreen wasn't sure if Clara had her own purpose for coming out for a run or if she wanted to talk, so Doreen carried on her way but moved slower. When she heard her name called, she turned around and saw Clara with a frown on her face.

"You did have a reason for coming here, didn't you?"

Goliath wound through her legs, but Mugs barked a couple of times then just sat and stared at her.

Clara ignored them both. Her gaze stayed locked onto Doreen's face.

"Obviously you know I'm interested in cold cases," Doreen said simply. "I wonder at the circumstances of this one."

"It's hard to imagine your daughter's life being reduced to a cold case," she bit off, a little temper attached.

"I'm sorry." Doreen winced. "I didn't know your daughter, but I feel for both of you. I'm just getting to know who she was."

"She was a wonderful, bright, outgoing, bubbly young girl," her mother said warmly. "She wouldn't kill a spider. She'd pick them up to move them out to the bush."

"And how many people could possibly know where she slept?"

"Not very many," her mom said. "She'd just moved into that bedroom a couple months earlier. Her father had used it as an office before. When we divorced, I moved across the road so we could share custody of our daughter. She'd come back and forth but could still see both of us if she wanted to. It was not as common a methodology for divorced couples back then, but it was working for us."

"You have no idea who could have done this?" Doreen asked curiously.

"Her stepmother," Clara said. "Crystal and Mary never got along."

"Was Mary there the whole time?" Doreen asked.

"She moved in a few weeks after we separated," Clara said, her voice stiff. "And you'd think that, after all this time, I wouldn't care. But it still rankles."

"Of course it does," Doreen said, perfectly capable of understanding the woman's mind-set over being replaced. After all, that was exactly what had happened to Doreen. "What about friends, family friends, anybody you know who had a record or had any kind of suspicious or overly affectionate relationship with Crystal?"

The woman winced at that. "Honestly, in the previous months, it had been pretty rough. Nobody was coming by because of the divorce. I know Crystal complained bitterly that she had lost a lot of her friends because she couldn't have them over anymore, and that was causing some trouble with her and her father too."

"What was her relationship like with her father?"

"Very loving, very caring," Clara said gently. "It's one of the reasons why I moved across the road so we could both be involved in her life. Crystal loved both of us," Clara said. "And then Mary moved in, and I know Crystal was no longer as happy to be over there."

"Is Mary still there in that house?"

"With Eric? Yes."

"Did they go on to have any children of their own?"

"No," Clara said. "Neither have I. When you devote eight years of your life to the most precious thing in the world, and then somebody takes it from you, it's pretty hard to recover."

"I'm so sorry for your loss," Doreen said.

There was a moment of uncomfortableness while the woman nodded, her gaze searching Doreen's. "Do you think you can help?" she asked abruptly.

Doreen shrugged. "I don't know," she said as honestly as she could. "The fact that I've had beginner's luck looking into several of these cases gives people an overconfidence in my abilities."

"But that's not necessarily true. Besides, Mack is helping you too, isn't he?"

"Or I'm helping Mack," Doreen said with a chuckle. "He's not allowed to tell me much about any active cases. I can get the same information from witnesses myself though, and that helps. Of course I have a transcript of the TV show that was produced to try to find Crystal too."

Clara nodded absentmindedly.

"The footprint appears to be the biggest piece of evidence," Doreen said. "But it's not much to go on."

"The police thought I did it," she said abruptly. "And I immediately thought Mary did it."

"You're a nurse. I highly doubt you wear high heels," Doreen said. "But it's a great way to throw off the police's suspicions."

"Exactly, and Mary runs a clothing boutique downtown," she said. "She's always dressed up."

"Which would then make it obvious she was involved," Doreen said. "No, I highly suspect it isn't a female at all."

"You have to remember, or maybe you don't even know," Clara said, "Crystal was tiny. She was eight, but she was the size of a six-year-old. She would never be more than five feet tall. She was a beautiful china doll. And it still hurts so damn much."

"All I can say is that I'll look into her disappearance,"

Doreen said. "No guarantees though."

"I'm hoping your reputation is not based on beginner's luck," Clara said, "because I really, really want answers. But more than that, I want my daughter home again." Suddenly she burst into tears, whirled around, and ran back up the hill to her house.

That left Doreen standing here, awkwardly watching as Clara ran, her long legs eating up the block as if she were used to running. And, with that kind of stress, maybe jogging was an avenue that helped her to deal with her loss. Doreen didn't think she could deal with it anywhere near as well as Clara had.

Doreen turned slowly and headed back home again. "Well, guys, for better, for worse, it looks like we have ourselves another mystery. Because no way I can turn my back on poor Clara. And I especially can't turn my back on poor Crystal," she said.

Mugs woofed in agreement.

Chapter 12

Sunday Midafternoon ...

JUST BECAUSE DOREEN couldn't let anybody down didn't mean the answers would come. This was another case where she had to tread carefully. This was a recent case—well, okay, one from ten years ago that could be related to this recent case. Still, that put the original event in the cold-case category, but it wasn't like it was twenty or thirty years ago, where half the population of Kelowna didn't even know about it. Most likely, this case was still on everybody's mind. It was certainly still on Clara's.

Once back home again, the doors locked, Doreen headed to the kitchen and her trusty teapot. She had only sat down for five minutes before Mugs jumped up on his back legs before her. She looked at him and frowned. "Did I not feed you?" She promptly fed them all, watching as they buried their faces in their food.

Somehow she planned these walks for an hour, but they often became two. She should get a pedometer to track her footsteps. She imagined it would surprise her just how many thousands she'd taken in a day, and that could account for the fact that she still hadn't put on any of the weight she'd lost after separating from her husband.

Her husband would approve of this look. He had always preferred the bony hips and the thin shoulder blades and collarbones, like cover models. Doreen was actually putting on some muscle with her gardening work. When she thought about how she had manhandled a lot of the tools and done the gardening at Penny's place, she figured gaining muscle was a lot better than being skinny.

Just the thought of Penny brought a sense of disquiet to Doreen. She'd really liked the woman. But, when you find out all the secrets somebody is working hard to keep hidden, you learn a lot about the person behind it all.

Doreen was sorry she hadn't met George, who'd done something for his wife to keep her safe and had held that secret deep inside until it was like a poison, fearing every-thing bad that happened since then had been his fault. Doreen didn't have any right or wrong answers on fate or karma or good versus evil, yet she figured a lot of the evil came in the two-legged form.

As she sat quietly musing away, surprisingly tired, Mugs came to her and jumped up again on his back legs. She reached down and scratched his long ears. "What's the matter, boy?" He woofed a couple times and then walked back to the living room and turned to look at her. She frowned but got up and followed him.

Left behind, Thaddeus squawked and said, "Wait, wait, wait," and he dashed off the table to land on the floor with a hard *thump* and proceeded to waddle behind them. Goliath wouldn't be left alone either and sauntered forward. Doreen stood in the living room and stared at Mugs. "What's the matter?"

He barked several times.

She frowned and then realized with horror that he stood atop the hidey-hole entrance. She walked over to him and asked, "Really? Are you sure?" She kept her voice at a whisper.

He barked again and again.

She didn't know what to do now. If somebody was down there, they could have gotten in this way or from the garage—most likely from the garage, as coming in through the main doorways would have set off the alarms. But, once the intruder was down there, he could come up through here quite easily and then … what?

She glanced around at the antiques on the mantel and all around the property and realized she had almost no inventory of everything left here after Scott's moving men had packed up things, but it didn't take long to note a couple of items collected to one end of the mantle. But was that because Scott had set a few items aside for Agatha to look at? Or to go to Christie's? Or had the movers shifted things around so they didn't fall off and break with their movements? Swearing to herself, she backed up and walked through the kitchen, into the garage, where the double doors led down to the basement while dialing Mack. While passing through the garage, she picked up a pitchfork she'd gotten from Penny's and stood at the double doors, checking them out. There was no way to prop anything underneath those handles. They were lever-tight, and she wasn't sure she'd jam anything in there that would stop the intruder from opening these doors. When Mack answered the phone, she asked, "Are you busy?"

"Don't have to be. Why?"

"Because I think I have an intruder again."

He swore softly. "Don't go after him," he barked out as

a warning.

"Then you better get here fast," she said in a mutinous tone. "Because, if he's after my antiques, you know what I'll do to him."

"I'm coming. I'll be there in five minutes. Hold your horses."

"I will," she said, "but I'm not sure I can watch both entrances."

"Just hold on," Mack said in alarm. She heard his vehicle start up and grinned at that.

She wondered how to check the front entrance and this one to make sure nobody was at either spot. She walked back and forth from one to the other but, so far, saw no sign of anyone. Only Mugs wouldn't stop barking a warning bark.

"You keep warning him," she said, her voice rising. "I don't know who's down there, but that somebody should be prepared to take a pitchfork in the abdomen." She wasn't usually so feisty and had never been bloodthirsty, but something about people trying to take what wasn't theirs got her blood going.

She made another trip, heading back inside to check on the trapdoor in the living room floor. It was hard for one person, *her*, to keep an eye on both of the exits, so she pulled the two heavy pot chairs over the wooden trapdoor, hoping she'd at least hear if somebody tried to push open that hatch. *Oh, my God!* As a complete afterthought, she grabbed one of the kitchen table chairs and jammed it under the doorknob to the single door basement access also from the living room.

Then she raced back to the double doors in the garage, waiting for somebody to exit that way. Of course she hadn't opened either door and checked the basement for her intruder. Mack would have a heyday if she did. Some things he just wouldn't tolerate, but if he didn't know about it ...

Still, she didn't know if her intruder was one person or two people. Or more. She walked over to the big exterior garage door, unlocked it, and pulled the huge door up, amazed at the kind of lift-swing system that allowed her to manually lift the heavy door so easily. She had no idea such a thing was possible before. The garage doors in her previous home had looked heavy and awkward and completely impossible to move. She'd only had ones with remotes, yet she didn't even remember having that. Usually the doors were opened for her and closed after she was inside by somebody else. She hadn't even had to bother with remotes at her own home.

She shook her head as she realized just how completely useless she'd been before and how different her life was now. She stared down at her fingers and her fingernails, wincing. Her hands were scraped, the nails rough and ragged, and they were certainly not the long, pointed, manicured nails she used to sport.

They were also stained almost a light brown, as if she were a smoker. She rubbed her fingertips together, wondering where that discoloration had come from. It was hard to imagine which chemicals would do that, but nicotine was the worst. Or iodine. And she certainly hadn't had her hands close to either of those. Still, something in the local soil was reacting to her nails. Oh, well, ... such was her new, improved life.

She went back inside to check on the living room again, saw the pot chairs were still there and the kitchen chair still propped where she had left it, and came back out to the garage. That was where she was when Mack drove up.

Mugs raced toward Mack as he hopped out, took one

look at her, his gaze going to the pitchfork in her hand, and he slowly, carefully let out a hard breath. He strode forward and gently removed the pitchfork from her hand and hung it back up on the wall. Crouching down to greet an ecstatic Mugs, he turned to glare at her.

She motioned at the double doors leading downstairs and, in a low voice, said, "We went for a walk and came back. All the security was set. I sat down to have a cup of tea. Mugs here was kind of bugging me. I didn't understand what he wanted, so I fed him, and then, when he was done, he did the same thing again, and he led me back to the living room." She walked him inside where she'd put the pot chairs over the hatch and pointed to the kitchen chair at the single basement door too. "When I figured they didn't have to come in through the alarms, and they could have come in through the garage because I don't have security everywhere."

Mack frowned, nodded, and walked back out to the double doors in the garage. With her staying at the top at his instruction, he slipped down the stairs and turned on the lights. She had to hold Mugs back. Mack stopped at the bottom step and took a long look, but he saw nothing. He turned to look up at her, and she pointed to the small room off to the side, the root cellar area. He nodded and tiptoed forward so he could look around the corner.

Mack disappeared from view while she watched and then listened. She heard a shout, various sounds followed by a kerfuffle, and no way could she could just wait here. What if he needed her help? She snatched the pitchfork off the wall again. With Mugs barking and urging her on, she raced down the stairs. As she came around the corner into the cold-room section of the basement, she found Mack with a man on the dirt floor, pinned under his knee.

She flicked on the light and smiled. "You got him," she cried out in delight.

Mack nodded, looked at her, and groaned. "Put that pitchfork back," he ordered. "And get Mugs to quiet down."

She lifted the pitchfork ever-so-slightly in defiance. "He was breaking into my house," she snapped. "If you weren't here, you know I would have taken my pitchfork to him." She squatted and placed a calming hand on Mugs.

Mack lifted the guy's head and turned it over so he could see Doreen with her pitchfork. "This is what you would have come up against," he said, "and that's the easy part."

The kid just groaned.

Mack lifted him up so he stood on his feet but had his arms pinned behind his back.

Doreen looked at her intruder and cried out, "I don't even know who you are. What are you doing in my house?"

He just stared at her and frowned.

"You're working with them, aren't you?" she snapped. "You're working with Darth."

The kid looked surprised when she brought up the name. He frowned and then shrugged. "He said he had left some stuff here, and you were trying to steal it from him."

She snorted at that. "He's in jail because he broke into my house and stole things from *me*," she stated. "And when did you have a chance to talk with him?"

The guy winced.

She crossed her arms, planting the pitchfork in the soft ground first. "Seriously? You were in jail when you talked to him? Well, that figures, doesn't it? Another lowlife."

"Hey, that's not fair," he snapped. "I was just going out to party and got a little too drunk."

"Yeah, sure. And just because of that you were really happy to turn around and pick up his dirty deed and carry it on, huh?"

"I needed the money," he whined.

"How would he pay you?" she asked. "He's in prison."

He just shrugged and stayed quiet. She looked at Mack. "Now what?"

"Now I have more paperwork again. Like you don't cause me enough paperwork," he growled.

"It's not my fault this time. ... Besides, it is what it is," she snapped, then returned her gaze to her intruder. "How did you get into my house?"

"The outside door to the garage," he said. "It's not locked."

"No," she said. "I was struggling with that earlier. I normally keep a chair propped underneath it."

"Sure, but when I gave the door a good shake, the chair fell to the side."

"Figures," she snapped. She stared at Mack.

He nodded. "I'll be glad when the antiques guy comes back to take that stuff."

"But that doesn't mean I'm in the clear," she said, "as I still have all the little stuff to deal with."

"You'll need to do something about that really fast," he said, "because obviously the word is out that your house is full of valuables."

"Drat," she said. She ran her fingers through her hair and sighed. "I need to do something. Maybe you can help me completely close that one garage door. Nail it shut. I don't know," she said. She straightened, looked in the direction of the door, and said, "Maybe I'll go look at that right now." She walked back toward the door, then stopped.

"Do you need help with him? Or are you okay to take him to the station?"

"I got this," Mack said as he pulled a pair of handcuffs from his back pocket, and, while she watched, he hooked the guy's wrists together. "I've patted him down. He doesn't have anything on him."

"Probably making a pile to take out later." She grinned at her intruder. "See? Crime doesn't pay. And you're going to jail *again*. That's what you deserve," she said triumphantly. "How dare you come into some poor woman's house and steal from her?"

"Hey," the guy said, "I don't have anything on me."

"Have you tried getting a real job?" she asked in a snide voice, holding Mugs close.

"No," he snapped. "Have you?"

She grinned and said, "I already work. Part-time, but at least I do." And she turned and walked away. She wouldn't tell him that she was working in Mack's mother's garden. Her intruder didn't have to know that detail.

Back up in the garage, she navigated around the furniture and walked over to the door in question. Sure enough, the chair had fallen to the side. Frowning, she picked it up, opened the door, closed it a couple times, and wondered what she was supposed to do to secure this door. It wasn't like she had much in the way of spare wood to put over it and to nail it closed. And, if she did the same on the outside, what would stop anybody from pulling the boards off there too?

The door opened outward, and, of course, lovely Hornby had shaved it down so it was easy to open. Too easy to open. She studied the bottom, wondering if she could jam something underneath to stop it from opening, but it would have to be cleverly concealed to stop anybody else from getting in. She made her way back into the kitchen and grabbed a cardboard box, and, with her trusty scissors, headed back out to the garage. She cut off one flap from the box and folded it and, using a crowbar, jammed it really tightly underneath her unsecured door, so it was almost impossible to see.

When Mack came up with his prisoner, she walked over and said, "Do you want to try opening that door for me?"

He shoved the thief into a kitchen chair and told him to sit. With Doreen standing guard with her trusty pitchfork, Mack tried the door. He looked back at her and raised an eyebrow.

She beamed at him. "Now I think we might be safe."

He shrugged and said, "Well, it's good. Could put a couple spikes through here too, but it's not likely the best idea. It'll crack the core of the door. This is pretty tight." He motioned at his prisoner to get up and said to Doreen, his voice raspy, "We'll talk about how you handled this later."

She just beamed at him. "Whenever." She walked both of them to Mack's car as he seat-belted the guy into the back seat. She stood there, frowning at Mack. "I don't think you should take him alone."

"He's not going anywhere," Mack said, "I'll lock him in. We have a cage behind my seat. I'll be fine." But he grinned at her. "Nice to know you care." Then he remembered something and pulled a roll of small bills from his pocket. "Before I forget again, here's your gardening money."

"Thanks." Happily she took it and stuffed it in her pocket, but then her frown returned as she looked at the punk kid in the back seat, smirking at her. "I don't like his attitude," she announced. The punk's smile fell away. She felt better after that.

Then the punk glared at her and said, "I don't like your attitude either," mimicking her voice. Again she just glared at him and watched as the two left.

Mugs lay at her feet, seemingly content.

Chapter 13

Sunday Late Afternoon …

NOW THAT DOREEN was alone again and her house empty of unwanted persons, she couldn't rest until she did a thorough check through everything. She should have had Mack check the whole house. What if somebody had come out from one entrance while she and Mack were at the other?

After a quick search starting upstairs and working her way downstairs, Doreen noted that her animals seemed unperturbed. Feeling better, Doreen locked up the external doors again—along with the unsecured garage door now jammed tight, the big external garage door shut and locked, the internal kitchen door shut and locked and with a kitchen chair jammed under its knob—and she then set the security. She stood in the middle of the living room and brushed her hands together.

"There," she said, "that should fix it." By now it was nearing dinnertime. She was tired and fed up and oddly pissed off that somebody else was trying to steal her antiques. She had to get through today on her own, guarding her pricey collections, and then tomorrow she'd be fine, once

Scott got here in the morning. The moving guys would be here again for those big-ticket items, but she really needed somebody to sell these little items.

On that note, she walked over to her laptop, turned it on, and sent a note asking if Scott could remember to send her the names of other experts she could contact. Not expecting to hear from him anytime soon, she sat down and browsed the internet, looking for local shops. Mostly boutique clothing stores popped up.

Places that she would have normally loved, but considering boutiques were almost always more expensive ... She didn't need any clothes. She still had a massive stack in the spare room to sort through.

When her stomach rumbled, she stood, looked in the fridge, and frowned. Deciding to be good, she made a salad and opened a can of tuna, mixed it with mayonnaise, and dabbed it around the top of her lettuce. For an added touch, she then took a dill pickle, chopped it up, and added it to the center.

Taking her plate outside, she sat in the waning sun, watching the backyard with all her animals around her. It was just so peaceful and relaxing when she could see the water at the edge of her property gently flowing toward the lake with the late afternoon sunlight dappling across the ripples. The sun at this particular height and strength made all the green grass look so much brighter, all the yellows so much more golden.

As soon as she finished her salad, she made a cup of tea and then walked with her critters down to the creek. She considered the area and really wanted a bench so she could sit here and enjoy the view.

In lieu of a bench, she chose a couple rocks along the

water's edge. Slipping off her sandals, she sat down, letting her feet rest in the water. It was still early in the year. She wasn't sure when the spring runoff would happen. So far, the water just trickled by, although, as she looked around, she frowned because several of the rocks that she used to be able to see were now under water. So the water *was* rising. Had it been rising steadily, and she just hadn't seen it happen? All too possible. She had been a little busy.

Sometimes spring came very early and sometimes late. There just didn't seem to be any rhyme or reason. But then maybe global climate change was having an effect here …

She imagined living along the river would be different each and every year because Mother Nature never did anything exactly the same.

There was a bit of a slope from the edge of her property down maybe a foot and a half or so. As she stopped and really looked at it though, she found it was a good two feet. And this little backyard garden sloped up toward the house, so that was probably another foot or two. How high did the water rise at this area? The creek itself wasn't terribly wide here, so it would probably come through pretty fast and sharp. Maybe that was why the old back fence had been beaten up. Maybe the spring runoff hit it year after year, and the battering over time just made it all go to pieces. It wasn't her current issue, but she sat here and found the water level high enough now that the ducks could swim past her place. She sat entranced as a mallard pair went by, followed by several goldeneyes. She couldn't believe how beautiful they were and how completely uncaring Mugs was, sitting here beside her. She put a hand on his neck in warning. "We leave all of Mother Nature alone," she said in a firm voice. But, true to Mugs, he turned and looked at her and raised an eyebrow as if to say, *Who are you kidding?*

He had been instrumental in dealing with intruders and people attacking her, so she amended her warning to say, "We leave all of Mother Nature's animals alone, except for the nasty two-legged ones."

He sagged down so he lay stretched out, but he was ever alert while he watched the antics of the ducks as they dabbled along the far edge of the creek.

Goliath was the one that worried her now. He sat on a rock, staring at the ducks, his body in a pounce position, the rough of his neck alert, and he made weird little sounds in the back of his throat while his tail twitched hard.

"Goliath," she said in a stern voice. "That's a no."

His tail just flicked at her once really hard as if to say, *Yeah? And who'll stop me?*

She studied the distance between the ducks and Goliath and noted that, unless he got over his disgust of water, the ducks would be perfectly safe.

And, of course, Thaddeus, not to be outdone, sat on a rock beside Goliath, calling out, "Good afternoon, Thaddeus here. Good afternoon, Thaddeus here."

She chuckled. "I don't think they can talk back like you talk," she said, laughing at the bird's antics. She picked up her phone and put it on Video. "Say hello again, Thaddeus," she cried out.

Thaddeus looked at her and snapped his beak shut.

"Why do you insist on being perverse?" she asked in exasperation. "You know how perfect it would be to see you introducing yourself to the ducks? Maybe they didn't hear you the first time," she tried again.

He cocked his head, looking at her as if she was full of it.

And, of course, she was talking to the dratted bird as if

he were a child. Still, he acted that way a lot of the time, so maybe she wasn't so far off. The ducks finally paddled their way farther up the creek, leaving her without any other wildlife to enjoy. She shifted position until she could lean back against another rock and closed her eyes, her face up against the setting sun. She could hear the birds above the beautiful willow on the other bank. She sat here, enthralled. "Good thing I didn't bring that loser of a husband here," she murmured. "He'd never appreciate such simple joys as this."

"Good thing, isn't it?" a familiar voice asked.

Startled, she turned to look at Steve, Penny's lawyer friend. He glared at her. And suddenly she realized just how exposed she felt. Vulnerable even. "You got a problem?" she asked defiantly. Where did she learn a good defense was a strong offense? Because really that would be a bad idea here. Mugs growled as he turned his attention to the approaching stranger.

"It's okay, Mugs," she whispered. And she hoped it was. But she couldn't guarantee it. Steve looked at her with one of those *I hate what you've done to my life* looks.

"Sorry you've lost your friend." She spoke calmly but kept him in her sights. "If Penny hadn't tried to kill me, she would have had one less criminal act to worry about."

"You're the only one who says she tried to kill you," he scoffed. "She told me that she did no such thing, and you fabricated the entire lie."

She stared at him. "I still have stitches in my head," she said indignantly. "She hit me over the head with a pry bar, for crying out loud."

He just shrugged and said, "That injury needing stitches could have come from anywhere."

"I wasn't alone. There was a witness," she said. "Or have

you forgotten that?"

"Penny said he arrived after the fact, and you're the one who told him what she'd done."

She was a little worried Penny could turn Doreen's story around that way, but she shook her head and said, "No, that's not true. But then I'm not going to sit here and argue with you regarding something you know nothing about, which you didn't witness yourself. Obviously you care very deeply for her, and again I'm sorry for your loss." Then she stood, knowing she should probably leave well enough alone. But, unable to do that, she said, "On the other hand, maybe you should be thanking me."

He stared at her.

"Well, you've got to be thinking how every male around Penny was murdered," she said quietly. "Or at least died under suspicious circumstances."

His face darkened, and he took a threatening step toward her. Immediately Mugs placed himself in front of her and growled. Steve looked at the dog in disgust. "If you think that little upstart will stop me when I really feel like going after you," he said, "you can think again."

"So that's a threat, is it?" she asked, remembering her phone was still on Video in her hand. She tilted her cell phone screen to show it to him. "Would you care to repeat that?"

"I don't have to repeat anything," he said. "You'll get yours. I promise." He turned around on his heels and walked away.

She held up her phone, making sure she got a good picture of him as he left. Then she squatted, her hands shaky, her stomach queasy, as she cuddled Mugs. "Thank you, big guy. He might have dissed you, but I do believe he didn't want to take you on."

Goliath wove between her legs to come up between her and Mugs, looking for ear scratches. As Doreen looked around to see where Thaddeus was, he waddled after Steve, the guy who'd just threatened her. "Thaddeus, come back here," she called out.

Thaddeus turned, looked at her, and cocked his head. She patted her knee as if he were a dog. "Come on. Let's go back inside and get treats."

At that, Thaddeus lifted his wings and half-ran, half-hopped toward her in a weird flightless movement. She bent down, scooped him up, and put him on her shoulder. As she straightened, Steve had disappeared from sight. That was oddly even more disquieting.

Back in the house, she reset the security and sat down in the living room, just to relax a bit, but, feeling restless, she decided to grab a bottle of water and moved the animals upstairs, and then realized she'd forgotten to give them their treats. She raced back down, grabbed the treats, and then gave them to the animals in her bedroom. She looked at the room and groaned. "There's still so much stuff. Nan, why?"

But with still an hour until her normal bedtime, she had time to do more. She had stacks of clothing on the floor which she sorted through, laughing when she realized the entire stack could go to Wendy. She likely needed another box and another bag, considering the number of shoes and belts and scarves. They just weren't her style—some were very western looking; some were full of rhinestones; some were beaded things that she didn't understand.

She stuffed a lot of the items in the one empty box in her bedroom. She went down to the kitchen, grabbed a large garbage bag, brought it back up, and filled it completely.

Groaning, she headed back downstairs, grabbed a second one, came back up, and had it full soon too. But at least that stack on the floor was gone. As far as she was concerned, that was enough for the night.

The animals agreed because they sat on her bed, already half asleep, and she remembered she had still not found anything for Thaddeus to sleep on. "Darn," she said. Noting the hook in the ceiling for draping a hanging lamp, she wasn't sure just what she could do, but she had a really big rectangular scarf hanger—Nan loved her scarves apparently—about four feet long, with one bigger round section at the bottom where Thaddeus could perch. That might work. Climbing on a sturdy chair, she hung it from the hook on the ceiling.

When she jumped back down, she studied her new roost for Thaddeus. The biggest ring was really thin and would be hard on his claws. He'd have to hold on really tight. Not sure he could even do that. So she grabbed a couple of the scarves and wrapped them around the biggest ring, turning it into a padded perch. Now he had something bigger to hold on to, and it was soft enough to not hurt him.

And the best part was, she could reach him on it without a chair.

Thaddeus had watched her curiously as she started and finished this project. When she scooped him up and placed him on it, he squawked several times and then moved around a little bit from side to side as if assessing the best place to sit. Then he lowered himself and perched.

She looked at him and smiled. "I know it's not quite big enough," she said apologetically. "And it's definitely rustic looking, but I promise we'll find something else for you soon." She gently stroked his cheeks. He pushed his head in as he cuddled her fingers. She got on her tiptoes to kiss him gently.

As she stepped away, he pooped onto her floor.

Forgot the dang newspaper. Such was her life.

Chapter 14

Sunday Evening...

"REALLY?" SHE ASKED Thaddeus. "Did you just do that after I made you this nice new perch?"

Doreen looked around, but she had no newspapers up here. There should have been some nearby, but she'd cleaned them all out the last time she'd cleaned up his mess. Once again, back downstairs to Nan's trusty stack of papers. She returned, cleaned up his most recent mess, then put a folded newspaper underneath him, and stored the others off to the side. Needing to clean the room out a little bit now that she had made space for him, she took the bags of clothing to the top of the stairs and then pushed the box there too, so it was all stacked up in the same place.

"It's not much," she said out loud, "but it is something. Maybe in the morning I can get up and do the rest. Wouldn't that be nice? To have this room completely cleaned out?"

On that thought, she had a quick shower and headed to bed.

When she woke in the morning, she felt rested. Stronger. More at peace. Then Steve's visit last night came sliding back into her consciousness, and she could feel herself stiffening with tension all over again.

She wondered if she should mention it to Mack. It seemed more alarmist than common sense, but, if anything did happen to her, he wouldn't have a clue where to start looking.

Knowing he would be more than pissed at her if something *did* happen to her and she had not shared this with him, she uploaded the video to an email and sent it to Mack with a note, **If I disappear ...**

Chuckling, she got dressed and headed to the kitchen. It was Monday. Today Scott was coming, and she couldn't be happier. Today she'd be rid of all the big furniture—hopefully. Downstairs, her usual coffee made, she looked at the stove and wondered about an omelet—still the only thing she could cook confidently. She wasn't super hungry, but the salad last night hadn't been very substantial. Making a decision, she created a simple cheese omelet. She had to smile at her successful adventure. She didn't know how long Scott would be here, and another round of moving out the antiques could be quite stressful, particularly for the animals. Given that, she fed them first, then sat down to eat.

With her first bite, her phone rang.

"What the hell was that all about?" Mack snapped into her ear.

When she could swallow the bite in her mouth, she explained. "Well, he threatened me, and I realized I probably hadn't said very much about him, and so, if something happens to me," she said, "you wouldn't have any clue where to go looking for the guilty party." She thought about it, then added, "It just seemed like common sense to send it to you. Sorry if it seemed a little over-the-top." Of course, if she got a rise out of him, good.

It was never good for Mack to get too complacent around her.

"Yes, of course, it's common sense to send it to me," he said, his voice tired. "And I'm not mad that you sent it. I'm mad that it happened in the first place."

"I understood him to be an old friend of Penny's," she said, "and I don't know what that means in this instance. But he's obviously angry about what happened to Penny, and Penny is obviously trying to use the argument that we faked her attacking me."

There was silence on the other end, and Mack laughed. "It's a good thing we have photos of the wound matching up with the murder weapon—or the attempted murder weapon—that you couldn't possibly have hit yourself with. It couldn't even have fallen off one of your racks and hit you with enough force to cause that kind of damage."

"Plus you saw me, right?"

"Yes," he said, "I came out while she was attacking you. No way she'll get off on that charge."

Doreen felt some of her tension ease back. "Well, she certainly has Steve believing her story, so I'm sure a lot of people will. I'm the upstart. She's the one who's been here forever."

"And murdered her own brother," he reminded her. "Tried to kill Hornby."

"Sure, but look at the circumstances," she said gently. "You know a lot of people will have sympathy for her. Most will understand why she did what she did. And shooting Hornby ..." She stopped and frowned. "Nobody liked him anyway."

"True," he said thoughtfully. "On that note, we should

probably do a reenactment, so we have a video for a court trial."

"What does that mean?"

"It means I want you to come into the station today, and we'll take more pictures so the guys can put it through reconstruction software and show how it happened."

"Okay," she said, "but not until after Scott arrives, and only if he doesn't need me."

"Right," he said. "That should be today too."

"Absolutely, at least I haven't heard anything different. And I really need this stuff gone," she said fervently.

"What about the little stuff?"

"I'm not sure," she said, "I sent Fen an email last night, looking to see if he knows anybody else who can recommend a buyer for some of these items."

"And what about your Scott guy? Can he give you names?"

"I have no clue," she said. "He told me that he would send me some names, but that hasn't happened yet. He's pretty excited about the gold mine he's found here. Maybe he's just too distracted."

"Do you know how many pieces he has taken?"

"No clue. Besides he's hopefully taking dozens more today. But that reminds me. The other two chairs haven't been picked up yet." She frowned. "And he didn't give me the contact information for them."

"He's coming this morning, so maybe you can get that to happen today too."

"Right," she said, "because five hundred dollars is five hundred dollars."

"Is that what someone's paying for two chairs?" he asked in surprise.

"Yes. That's the deal Scott made. Honestly, I don't know what I would do with just two chairs. And that'll leave me with literally two chairs left."

"If need be," he said in that casual male *we can do anything* attitude, "we can do a dump run."

"Right," she said. "Also do you have a place in town where I can drop off chairs like that? Like a church bazaar or something where people can come and get stuff they might need?"

"Sure," he said, "a lot of charities around here might pick that up from your house."

"Really?" she asked. "That would be awesome because then I don't have to fit all this stuff into my car. I already have bags and boxes to take to Wendy's again."

He laughed. "Will you ever get done with that master bedroom?"

"It's almost there," she said. "I've got everything out of the closet, but now I could use a dresser and maybe a set of shelves."

"We took out a set of shelves already from the master closet that were pretty well stuffed with all kinds of junk, but, if you want it back in there, we can move it back."

"I'll think about it," she said. Just then she heard vehicles. "Hey, I've got to finish eating before Scott gets here."

"What are you eating?"

"A cheese omelet," she said triumphantly. "And a piece of toast and fresh coffee."

"Wow, okay, so that's just mean," he said. "I missed breakfast."

She could now hear voices. "I gotta go," she said. "It sounds like they're here."

She hastily took a couple more bites as she waited for

people to come up the front steps. She still had half an omelet in front of her, and that didn't look like something she wanted to warm up later. She put it on top of her piece of toast and cut it in half. Now it looked like an egg sandwich, and she walked to the front door, munching on it.

She opened the door to see the moving men with a massive truck backing up into her driveway. Scott looked at her and smiled.

She waved, finished her sandwich half, and, realizing they would still be a bit, raced back to the kitchen, and picked up the other half. She gobbled it down in four bites and moved her dishes to the sink. She washed her hands and went back out front.

Scott was propping open the front screen door. Mugs was out on the driveway, making a nuisance of himself. She called him over, and he came back, woofing and barking, his tail wagging. "Since when did you become such a social dog?" she asked him. He just woofed some more. Scott called out a few of the men's names. She recognized a couple of them. They grinned at her and said, "I guess we're back for more."

"Lots more apparently," she said in a laugh. "I'll be happy when the house is empty."

"I can imagine," they said. Inside, Scott stopped in the living room, looked at the two chairs, and said, "Did those chairs not get picked up?"

She shook her head. "No, and you didn't leave me the buyer's contact information."

He picked up the two chairs and put them beside her pot chairs under the window. "These aren't going," he said to his moving men and motioned and pointed to the other chairs, then pulled out his phone and called somebody.

"Hey, are you not taking those two chairs? Today's Monday, and you said you'd come over the weekend."

Doreen heard a whiny voice on the other end but couldn't make out the words.

Scott shook his head. "This morning or they're gone," he said, and he hung up. He looked at her and said, "If he doesn't take them, I will. I might get a better price anyway."

She smiled up at him. "Can you take the other two?"

"I'll see what we have room for. I can only really take what I know we can sell, so that's the priority."

Many of the pieces were smaller this time, but they still required a lot of wrapping, and, by now, the moving men were working in shifts. With the garage door open and the bigger pieces already wrapped and put in the moving truck, she stepped back and watched the organized chaos in amazement.

When Scott came to find her an hour later, she was in the kitchen, doing research on Crystal.

"Doreen?"

Startled, she turned to look at him and hopped up to her feet. "Hey."

"The guy who wants those two chairs is here."

She nodded and said, "Good. It's five hundred dollars, right?"

Scott handed her the five hundred in cash and said, "That's yours, and I've given him the two chairs."

"Perfect," she said, loving the feel of that much money in her hand. She folded it up and tucked it into her purse with the other money, just now realizing how wealthy she was becoming. At least, for her, it was wealthy. It also reminded her about going to the bank. And she couldn't have been more grateful. She motioned to the coffeepot and said, "Would you like me to put on a fresh pot?"

His eyes lit up, and he nodded. "And then I'll go back out and work on the garage. We've got to get a lot of that stuff before we head down to the basement."

"There's no room to haul the basement furniture through the garage if you don't clean out the garage first."

He nodded, but he was back a moment later and said, "There's a woman at the door looking for you."

Surprised, Doreen headed out to her front steps.

There was Clara.

"Hi, surprised to see you here."

"I know," Clara said, "and obviously it's a really bad time. I'm on my way into work. I just wondered if you'd found out anything about Crystal."

Doreen was overcome with guilt. Not only had she not found very much but she hadn't put too much effort into it. She shook her head. "No, not yet," she said. "Sometimes it can take time."

Clara's face fell. "I know," she said. "I just figured that you being as good as you were …"

Feeling that was more than a little unfair, and yet, hating to disappoint a bereft mother, Doreen motioned to the moving men and said, "I'm also involved in a lot of things right now that cut into my time, and I do want privacy for the work I have to do," she said, her voice lowering at the end.

"I'm sorry. I didn't even think of that," Clara said, glancing around. "It's not exactly something you can do as part of a tea session, is it?" She backed down the steps to get out of the way of the men.

Doreen followed them as they moved out more stuff from the dining room, remembering the fragile china dishes.

She called out, "Those dishes aren't wrapped. They're just the way you guys put them in there the last time."

The men nodded and said, "We have special boxes for these."

At that, Clara said, "Look. I'm sorry. I didn't mean to intrude." Backing up over the grass, she added, "I'll talk to you later."

"Actually," Doreen said, speaking softly, "I need a picture, but most helpful would be an aged version of what Crystal would look like now. Do you have any photos of her? I know she's grown up now and will look very different but it would be something. And also a picture of your ex-husband and his new wife." Doreen was hoping to scan those in and then ask Google to find more matching images online. It was a thought anyway.

Surprised, Clara said, "Oh, my goodness, yes, of course. That's foolish of me. Of course you need those things. I can access them at work. I'll email some of those photos."

"Did she have any favorite toys, and did they go missing at the same time?"

Clara stopped, looked at her, and said, "Yes, she did. How did you know?"

Doreen didn't say anything, but it made sense. The problem was, only toys had disappeared so far in this other child's case, and that made her more than a little worried. "Like a teddy bear, a little doll? Do you have any photos of those?"

Clara hesitated. "I don't know," she said honestly. "But I can look."

"Good. And, in that email, write down anything you know about what disappeared with her. The clothing she had on, if her pillow went, whatever toys went, if she had a little-girl purse, anything." She wrote down her email on a notepad and handed it to her.

Clara, obviously reassured that Doreen was taking this seriously, gave her a bright smile and said, "I will, and thank you." She dashed down the driveway, getting around the big truck and into her small red car.

Doreen stood in the doorway, staying out of the way of the moving men as they carried box after box from the dining room. She walked down after the last one and watched as they carefully repackaged the dishes into boxes meant specifically for china. She was amazed at the care they took.

"You see? This is why you need to take these dishes," she said, pointing. "Because I wouldn't have taken anywhere near this kind of care."

They grinned at her. Just then somebody came up from the basement, and he had a big box of silverware.

He put it down, and she smiled. "It's hard to imagine those things cutting centuries' worth of food, isn't it?"

At that, he nodded and pulled out a velvet box for all the silverware as well, each one having separate slots and sections for each type of utensil. She watched in appreciation, pulling out her phone, asking the guys, "Do you mind if I take some photos of this?"

They shook their heads as she filmed them packing up the china and the silverware. They had just finished when one of the couches and the pot chairs were brought out directly from the garage and down the driveway. They were loaded into the back of the truck, then a dining room table went on top with more chairs above it. She grinned in delight, knowing part of the garage was already empty. But she also realized it would take time to finish the move. She caught sight of Scott talking to somebody. "Scott, you didn't give me the name of someone to check out the smaller items in the house."

"No," he said. "I have somebody coming here to meet us today." He looked at his watch and just then a white SUV-slash-van combo she'd never seen before drove up and parked in front of her house. She looked at Scott, who nodded, when he saw the tall gangly woman walking up the sidewalk all in black. Scott stepped forward. "Agatha," he said, shaking her hand. "This is Doreen."

Agatha looked at Doreen, her face not breaking a smile. But she shook her hand politely enough.

Scott said, "Let's come on inside and take a look." They walked back to the house and stepped inside.

"I also have somebody coming over to look at the books," Doreen said.

"Today?" Agatha asked.

"I believe so." She looked at Scott, and he nodded. "John's coming, isn't he?"

"He was supposed to come earlier, but he got delayed."

Agatha stopped in the living room, her gaze going from object to object to object, landing on various knickknacks on the wall, and then on the mantel. She picked up the blue vase, tilted it over, studied the impression underneath, and smiled. "This would fetch a decent penny. This is probably ten, maybe fifteen thousand right here."

Doreen gasped, then held her breath, as Agatha shook it ever-so-gently and then carefully upended the contents. Scott and Doreen chuckled. "We found those in there last time," she said. "We were looking for a way to hold them. We thought they were marbles, but they're too big."

"They are, indeed, too big," Agatha said, rolling them

around in her fingers. "But I have seen such things before." She put them down along with the vase on the mantel and picked up the small clock beside it.

And that started it. She went over piece by piece. By the time she had examined everything in the living room, she turned to Doreen and said, "Do you have anything else?"

Mutely, Doreen led the way into the dining room. The guys had moved all the boxes of china, but still there were pictures and candlesticks on the wall. Agatha beelined for the candlesticks, nodded when she checked a few things underneath, and muttered when she disconnected one from the wall and checked underneath. She turned to look at Doreen. "These are sixteenth century. We'd be more than happy to sell them through Christie's."

Doreen's jaw dropped at that. "But they're just candlesticks."

At that, Scott chuckled. "Doreen likes contemporary stuff," he said by way of explanation to Agatha. She caught the moment of disgust in Agatha's gaze before she shuttered it away.

Doreen felt she had to apologize. "I'm sorry," she said. "I just don't have any appreciation for this stuff, so I'd much rather not have it around. I don't want to damage it. Somebody else will enjoy it much more than I will."

Agatha nodded. "This painting as well," she said, "and those two paintings. Those two are a matched set, and this one is a well-known French painter from the early 1900s. The three of them will fetch a very nice price."

"I hate to ask, but what's a *very nice price*?"

Agatha looked at the three paintings, shrugged, and said, "Probably one hundred thousand."

Doreen, her hand to her chest, sagged against the wall.

"Are you serious?"

Scott shrugged and said, "This is why you shouldn't listen to me when it comes to items I'm not an expert in. I didn't think they had any value."

At that, Agatha burst out laughing. "So far, they are the most valuable things in the house."

"Except for the books," Doreen said apologetically. "I think Scott said they're more valuable."

Agatha turned to look at Scott. "Really?"

He nodded slowly. "I think so. But we'll have to wait for John to be sure."

Chapter 15

Monday Late Afternoon ...

DOREEN WAS A little overwhelmed—make that incredibly overwhelmed—by the time both Scott and Agatha left, both promising they would return on the next day because they hadn't brought in supplies for the paintings to be packed up properly. The moving men had cleared out the bulk of the furniture. There was a little bit of extra room, and Scott was still muttering about pieces. They hadn't planned on it being a two-day job again, but she didn't understand how he couldn't have. Last time it had been a two-day job, and they had picked up a lot fewer pieces. Or maybe he thought these smaller pieces were less valuable.

She didn't know. It was just too crazy.

Instead of getting anything accomplished like she was supposed to, including making a trip to the bank to get that cash deposited or making a trip to see Mack for his enactment, she'd spent all day going over the house. She'd taken photos and written down notes, and paperwork had exchanged hands.

She closed the front door, walked into the kitchen, and made herself that ever-lovely cup of comfort-tea.

She walked out to her back garden, where she collapsed onto the grass. Lying prone, stretched out to her full length, in the late afternoon sun, the animals wandered all over her—Mugs looking for attention, Goliath refusing to take no for an answer and lying from her belly to her chest, and Thaddeus, who appeared to think her head should be a perch. Finally he gave up and walked up and down her arm.

She groaned. "Today was … nuts. Good thing I had a good night's sleep because I'm feeling more than a little bit exhausted."

The trouble was the money. Like, *big, big money.* She knew that if she could make it to the point when all of this was sold, if any of their promises turned out to be reality, she should be fine, meaning, *financially secure.* With a certain amount invested, she could continue to live without having to worry about getting a full-time job. She would still need to do small gardening jobs, and she was fine with that. It wouldn't be the lifestyle she had been accustomed to, but then she no longer wanted that sterile perfection that was just an illusion.

She much preferred the reality of her current life. Right now, she lay full-length on the grass, and that was something she'd never have been allowed to do with her husband. There would have to be lawn chairs taken out onto a little patio and blocks laid out for her to walk on so as not to walk on the grass—oh, the outrage if she had walked across the grass itself.

There were a lot of similarities between her ex and the gardener at Rosemoor, for that matter. She lay here, rubbing her tired eyes, and yet, she was still so wired from everything she and the experts had discussed today, from books to furniture to paintings. Agatha was thrilled now that she'd found several of the paintings that she wanted to take back with her. There had been one in the spare room upstairs. The painting had some faint, weirdly lit picture of a little rowboat and a stream with a dock and various trees. It was kind of pretty, but it wasn't anything special—except Agatha had almost moaned in joy over it. Obviously that one was going. Two in her bedroom were going too. She didn't know if there were more downstairs in the basement. She hadn't even had a chance to look. The garage was mostly cleaned out. Some of the furniture had been brought up from the basement and into the living room.

And then there had been Clara's visit ...

"I'm also seriously tired," she said, yawning. Her phone rang. She groaned, picked it up, looked at it, and sighed. "Hi, Mack," she said, putting it on Speakerphone and laying it on the grass beside her. "I hope you don't have anything too difficult to ask. I'm laying down outside, absolutely done."

"Are they finished?"

"I don't think so," she said, rubbing her eyes again. "I am though." Just then Goliath shifted on her belly. "*Ump.*" He rolled over, stretched out a paw, and gently patted her lip with his claws. "We're all done. I'm lying on the grass. Goliath is on my chest. Mugs is lying on my shoulder, and it seems like Thaddeus is still getting comfortable. But, as far as Scott and Agatha, they're coming back tomorrow."

"Who's Agatha?" Mack asked.

"Another specialist," she said, "and John was supposed to come, but he couldn't get the red-eye he wanted apparently. So he'll be here tomorrow too." She groaned. "I can't believe how much having all those people in my space has just finished me."

"But did they take anything?" he asked in surprise. "I didn't think it would take that long."

"It was a slow process. I think they have most of it packed up, so they shouldn't be here all day tomorrow. But I do feel bad because Clara showed up at my door today, and she's really putting way too much stock in me," Doreen said, her earlier worries reappearing. "I hate that. She's hoping I can pull off a miracle, and I can't."

"Take it easy," he said. "Nobody is expecting you to pull off a miracle, but you've had such great beginner's luck that, of course, people will hope you can get lucky again."

"Yes, but this is a child, and it's more recent than the other cases," she said.

"We also don't have any reason to suspect she's dead yet," he said. "I know that's the popular opinion after such a long time, but we're also seeing a ton of reports where other kidnapped kids have been kept captive or integrated into a family. Then, when they turn eighteen, they finally can either escape or are released in some way."

"In this case, Crystal would be eighteen now," Doreen said, rolling her neck and stretching out more. Goliath dumped his paw into her soft, tender lip again. She lifted his paw and put it on her neck, and immediately he stretched it back up and batted her nose. "I just don't have a clue where to even start looking."

"There's a reason why the police haven't solved the case yet," he said humorously. "I know you're making us look like absolute idiots here recently, but we do work hard at this. We have protocols we follow and trails we check right to the end. We haven't given up on this case."

"Nan will check at the retirement home too," she said.

"Why?" he asked, his voice sharp. "Does she know anybody who knows something?"

"I hope so," Doreen said, "because I doubt the creek or the lake has anything to offer this time."

At that, he laughed. "Have the animals met Clara?"

"Yes," she said, "they have. Clara suggested it was Mary, the husband's new wife, but then that's almost a standard accusation."

"Speaking from true life again?"

"I try to forget that aspect of my life. Yet I was thinking about your brother not too long ago. Has he said anything to you about my case against my lawyer? I hate to bug him as it's really not been all that long since he said he'd look into it."

"I know," Mack said. "I did talk to him the other day, and he said he's still working on it. He sounded much more positive about it but didn't want me to give you false hopes until he had proof."

"Anything positive would help right now," she said, yawning again.

"Are you sure you slept last night?"

"I thought so," she said, "but my research has been weird. Maybe my mind was working on all that when I should have been sleeping. Lots of little girls going missing. It makes no sense that the second case with that similar footprint would have just taken the child's toys."

"Unless ..." Mack's voice trailed off.

"I know, unless they intended to take the child at the same time and were interrupted or were planning to abduct the child at a later date."

"We did toss around the idea that maybe they were just after the toys, that maybe they had another child who needed toys, and that somehow somebody had seen these and thought they would be ideal. It would be an easy job, so why not?"

"Nah," she said, "that's too obvious. You can apparently pick up toys at secondhand stores really cheap."

"So what do you think is going on?"

"I think the toys were supposed to go with the child, and, for whatever reason, the child was left behind."

"Left behind?" he asked, his tone turning curious. "You mean, as in a choice?"

She sat upright, thinking about what she'd just said. "What if the child was chosen, and the toys were taken so the child would be more comfortable, but something happened to make them realize the child was not a good choice?"

Silence was heard on the other end. "It's certainly not out of the realm of possibility, but why wouldn't they have left the toys?"

"Maybe they took them first, maybe threw them out the window, and intended to grab the child and pick up the toys again on the other side."

"That's possible," he said, "and what kind of scenario can you possibly envision where the child didn't fit the kidnapper's choice?"

"All kinds of things come to mind," she said slowly, hating to even think about the term "good enough" because every child was perfect as far as she was concerned. But then she was biased because she didn't have any of her own. With half a smile at her own humor, she said, "What if the child was on medicine? What if the child was sickly? What if the child was meant to be a female and potentially was living as a male?" she said cautiously.

At that, Mack gave a strangled exclamation. "I can't say

we came up with any theory regarding children born with ambiguous genitalia," he said. "How many times has that happened?"

"Per my research? In today's day and age? More than you would expect," she said slowly. "People are choosing to let their children identify their true sex in whatever way they want. My other theory is maybe the parent was abusive, and the child could have been damaged, physically and/or mentally."

"Okay, I can see how some Good Samaritan would want to take the child out of there and save it. In which case they'd make a second attempt. But kidnappers? ... Still, there was some talk about abuse with Crystal," he said quietly. "So maybe that is what happened."

"Oh, now that's interesting. I didn't realize that," Doreen said, staring off at her house. "Clara is supposed to send me a list of what went missing with Crystal and the clothes she was wearing at the time. Clara feels Crystal's stepmother wanted to get rid of Crystal so she and Eric could have a better life without the baggage of children. You know that the two houses are across from each other, right?"

"What do you mean, the two houses?"

"Clara, when she moved out, moved across the road," she said. "So the houses literally face each other. This way her daughter could go back and forth and see both parents. Apparently the parents themselves were okay with that and thought it was an ideal situation but not the new girlfriend-slash-stepmom. They're married now. Clara said Mary wasn't a fan of kids."

"But Crystal was hardly a toddler, and, if they were living that close, then both parents would have their freedom because the other could look after the child while one went on dates or trips or whatever."

"In theory, yes," Doreen said. "Honestly I'm so tired, none of this is making any sense."

"What did the animals think of Clara?"

"Mugs didn't like her," she announced suddenly. "He barked at her several times and then backed away."

"Does that tell you anything?"

"She was fairly aggressive at that point because she was asking me what was going on, what with me taking a walk in her neighborhood. He didn't seem to react the same way when she came to the door this morning," she said, "but then it was chaos here. We had moving men in the living room, in the dining room, in the garage. There were trucks and vehicles all over the place. I was surprised Clara stopped."

"Look. You always seem to end up in trouble with this stuff," Mack said, "and I know you're feeling very sympathetic toward Clara, but you can't be sure she doesn't have a hand in her daughter's disappearance." He took a deep breath. "So I hate to say this, but don't be too trusting. Let's not let Clara turn into a Penny scenario."

Chapter 16

Monday Night ...

SO I HATE to say this, but don't be too trusting. Let's not let Clara turn into a Penny scenario. Doreen hated to consider such an idea, but, even hours later, it was hard to let go of Mack's words. Clara and Penny were nothing alike. Doreen took an evening cup of tea out to her garden and walked over to the creek. As much as she loved having it open for her own backyard, sometimes she liked to sit down a little farther against the neighbor's fence and just enjoy being alone without seeing her house.

And that was what she did now. She moved up a few steps toward where Steve had disappeared, hating that he'd been around her place. She sat down on a large stone backed up close to the old man's fence so she could sit comfortably cross-legged with her back supported and just enjoy the trickling water.

She let the information flow through her brain to see if anything would come up when Clara, true to her word, sent an email with photos and a list of items. The little girl appeared to be bubbly and happy with braids on the side of her head and a big smile on her face. She looked well-adjusted and, from the photo at least, didn't show any signs of abuse, but then abuse was an insidious thing that could often be hidden behind clothing or an unsmiling face. Unfortunately the victims were often unaware they were being abused, sometimes feeling they had done wrong, and would do anything to appease their tormentor, to make their abuser's life easier.

It sucked, but, when a child disappeared, one had to consider all the options—no matter how ugly. Clara had also given Doreen the full names, addresses, and work information of both her ex-husband and the girl's stepmother. Clara herself had never remarried, but she had had boyfriends. The question Doreen needed to ask was whether Clara had any boyfriends at the time of the abduction. Often predators would find the children and then insinuate themselves into the parents' lives so they could gain access to the child.

Wasn't that a horrible thought?

These thoughts had her up and pacing. She wandered the backyard until she couldn't stand not knowing, at which point she walked back inside to search through crimes involving children, understanding what other cases there were. When somebody wanted that child, the questions were: A) Did they want a child for a childless couple, paying them big bucks, or B) Did they want that child for themselves? Because those two end results carried completely different motivations. If Mary was getting rid of her stepchild, then Mary would want to kill, sell, or dispose of Crystal in some way so she'd never show up again, whereas, if somebody wanted the child for themselves, that opened up a different set of options. Maybe they wanted the child to join their existing family; maybe they were childless and couldn't afford to adopt; maybe they thought this child was having a terrible life and wanted to spirit her away; maybe there was a sexual motive, which seemed to drive most predators.

And how sad was that? It was such a depressing topic that, by the time she had spent an hour reading about this, she was more than a little pissed off and fed up.

There were too many cases like this to be found on the internet, and they were all sad.

She made some cheese and crackers and, instead of tea, just made a hot lemon drink and carried it up to bed. "Come on, guys. It's been a really crappy evening, but let's see if we can get through tomorrow, as that's another massive day."

She headed into bed, but she couldn't sleep. She tossed and turned as weird images came to her mind, wondering about the recent case and just why somebody would have decided to take the toys but not the child. She was really worried the parents hadn't taken this seriously and had left the child in the same bedroom. What if the intruder came back for a second attempt? She knew that shouldn't happen, but it was so hard to ignore. She sent Mack a text, asking him to confirm that the child was no longer sleeping in the same bedroom. Even though it was the middle of the night, she figured he'd see it in the morning.

Feeling better, she closed her eyes as his response came back. **Child has been moved.**

She grinned, realizing she and Mack had a connection that she hadn't fully appreciated. Not only were they both on the same page on these crimes but they both came from the same position—their hearts. And that felt great.

She had made a great friend, one she'd like to keep for a long time. She hadn't expected to find a man in her life, and really Mack wasn't, not in *that* sense. At least she wasn't prepared to go that way for a while. She was still burning with the pain of her broken marriage and the mental torment her husband had put her through.

But Mack was the complete opposite type of man. Sure, he laughed at her sometimes, and she had to admit now that he often had good reason. After all, her basic life experience was lacking—although she was catching up fast.

Even her mother never had anything to do with managing money. She was given credit cards, and everything else was all taken care of behind the scenes by someone else. Same with Doreen's husband. Doreen had never paid the bills—she was still struggling with that concept. And, since she'd moved here, she'd had a couple bills come in the mail that she wasn't sure how to pay. She figured she could take it to the bank and have them do it for her, or she could learn to do it online with a YouTube video perhaps, but she didn't have an online account. And she needed that, right?

So Doreen was supposed to contact Nan about all that, avoiding more laughter from Mack as she asked her stupid questions. With all this chaos, she'd forgotten about that discussion. She got up, grabbed a notepad, and jotted down notes. She needed to go to the bank, pay these bills, deposit cash, remember to not accept checks that could **BOUNCE**, writing the word in large bold letters, and then chuckled at herself.

All these thoughts of money connected with her earlier thoughts. Was the child sold? Unless they were trafficking in children or in white slave prostitution—which was an ugly thought but all too common unfortunately—then somebody must know something. Crystal had been so young and vulnerable. So really Doreen needed to find out if there'd been any strange men around or in Crystal's life? Doreen couldn't afford to be sexist. Were any strange men *or women* around who would have had contact with Crystal, particularly anyone who left right after the child's disappearance?

As Doreen considered this, she figured the world had gone to hell in a handbasket, then thought about the phrase. What exactly did that even mean? She groaned and returned to bed, rolling over to find a comfortable position, punched the pillow, and stuffed it under her head one more time.

And then she saw a light flicker in her window. She bolted upright. Mugs rolled onto his back, completely ignoring her, and snored again. She got up and crept to her window to see somebody with a flashlight in her backyard. She opened the window and called out, "What do you want?"

Instantly the light flicked out, but she could see a shadow racing away in the darkness. She stood here, frowning, then decided she would have another sleepless night worrying about an intruder after her antiques, especially now that she knew about the books and paintings downstairs too. Checking her phone—it was two o'clock in the morning—she groaned.

"I need a good night's sleep. I won't be able to take naps tomorrow with the moving men coming again." But she knew that, until she figured out what the intruder was doing in her backyard, she would never fall asleep again. She got out of bed, the animals with her, except Thaddeus, happy with his new perch upstairs, who just opened his eyes, looked at her, and then closed them. She stroked him gently and said, "You just sleep, buddy."

She headed out the kitchen door, propping it wide open so the cool evening air outside would help stabilize the heat inside. Nan's house had no air-conditioning—something

Doreen might have to look at down the road after all these antiques were sold and after she had an accounting of real money to look at, not just promises of real money.

With both Goliath and Mugs at her heels, she carefully walked down the garden path to where the intruder had been and stopped somewhere around the new bed she had weeded.

"So did I just disturb him making his way up to my house?" she whispered under her breath. She used her phone for a flashlight and checked the footprints. All soft ground was here, and there should definitely be footprints left. Unfortunately, from what she could see, there didn't appear to be any visible evidence.

Except she saw a smudge, like a footprint that had slid.

"What the devil is that?" She crouched beside it, holding the animals back because Mugs would walk across the print and destroy it. It was so damn hard to see, but she took several photos just in case and then, using some rocks, she squared it off a bit and framed the area so she could look at it closer in the morning.

She walked to the creek and studied it in both directions but saw nobody there. In her mind, she wondered if it was Steve. The shape of her most recent intruder had appeared to be a large male, but she had no way to know if it was Steve or not, and why would he even care to show up in her backyard at two in the morning? Unless he was planning on causing her some trouble. What if he'd planted something in her garden to make it look like she was a criminal?

With her mind now glomming onto that horrific concept, she realized just how easy it would be for somebody to make her look guilty of a crime. She groaned. "So that's why people keep fences up. Not to keep Mother Nature out but to keep the evil people out," she said with a heavy sigh. "And that really sucks too."

Tired, worn out, confused, and even more upset, she slowly dragged herself back up to bed with her animals. Goliath snuggled along her left arm, while Mugs curled up against her belly, and, with her arms wrapped around them both, she finally fell asleep.

Chapter 17

Tuesday Morning ...

WHEN DOREEN WOKE the next morning, she felt like her body was weighted down with troubles. She slowly got up, sat on the edge of her bed, and rotated her shoulders to try to loosen the tension. She remembered her middle of the night trip to her backyard, got up, and walked over to the window. It was hard to imagine what was down there, but the rocks were still there in the garden, exactly where she'd placed them.

She dressed quickly, headed downstairs, put on her morning pot of coffee, and walked out to the garden while her coffee dripped. She knew her place would be chaos again once the movers arrived and wanted a few moments to herself.

She stood at the bottom of the garden path and studied the smudge in the dirt, outlined by her special rock formation. She took several more photos of it. Whoever it was had stepped in the corner of the turned-over garden and had slipped downward, leaving a mark but nothing helpful or distinguishable, except to prove that she'd had a visitor.

She stood for a long moment, her mind trying to formulate ideas, but nothing came to explain this. Because, if her intruder had come across the grass—which he had; she had witnessed it from her bedroom window—surely there'd be visible tracks of his footprints in the dirt as well. But she found none—only here at the corner of the garden, as if he'd walked the edge of her path on the rocks, deliberately avoiding leaving any tracks.

Frowning, she turned and walked back to the house, the animals shuffling along at her side. Mugs perked his ears up, and he raced to the back door. She called out to him, "Hey, Mugs. What's the matter, buddy?"

But he barked and barked and jumped up on the kitchen door. She opened the door—although she'd had it propped open, but her chair had slipped off to the side.

Or it had had some help.

Hating the suspicion that was ever-present now, she pushed open the door, and Mugs raced across the hallway to the front door. She propped the back door open again with the kitchen chair and headed to the front door. Instead of something or someone suspicious, she found Scott and the moving truck here already. She opened the screen door in surprise. "I wasn't expecting you quite this early," she admitted.

"It's after eight," he said gently. "Did you get any sleep? You look like you had a bad night."

"I had a bad night," she said wearily. "But that seems to be the way of it these days."

"I'm sure protecting these antiques has been difficult," he said sympathetically.

"You have no idea," she said. "I've had so many break-ins and intruders. Even last night I had somebody in the backyard with a flashlight."

He stared at her in horror. "Seriously?"

"Yes," she said, "seriously. And how wrong is that?"

"Oh, dear," he said. "Well, let's get everything out of here, if we can today. Agatha is bringing a different vehicle with proper crating for the pictures."

"Good," she said. "What about John?"

Scott nodded. "John is coming with Agatha."

"Perfect," she said. "Please, take it all. I'd love for the thieves to come in and find the place empty."

And, at that, they propped open the front door, and the chaos began. She stayed out of the way as much as she could, even wondering if she should run down to the bank but hated to leave the animals alone with the doors wide open. She could take them in the car but not into the bank itself. Even as she was deciding, Agatha drove up and an older stooped man, with more of a dusting of fuzz than actual hair on his head, got out and walked toward Doreen. She met him on the front lawn out of the way of the rest of the chaos.

She shook John's hand. "Hi," she said. "Nice to meet you, and hopefully the trip here will be worth it."

He just smiled and said, "I've made a lot of trips that weren't worth it. It's nice to meet you in person." He looked at Agatha. "Besides, Agatha said she'd found several wonderful finds, and I know Scott already has. So I'm hoping you could pull another rabbit out of the hat and find some treasure for me too."

She smiled and said, "Well, I'm more than willing for you to see what there is, but I honestly can't tell you if they are originals or fakes. I don't know the difference."

He nodded and said, "That's the best attitude to have. Let's go take a look, shall we?"

She led the way back in, pausing to give Mugs a chance

to sniff around the newcomers and bark at them again. "I'm sorry. The animals are a little on edge," she said by way of explanation when Mugs still barked at them. "Just so many people are here now."

Agatha waved her hand. "The animals calmed down yesterday just fine. I'm sure it'll be okay. I have two specialists with me as well." That was the first time Doreen noticed the two men behind her. "They'll help pack up the paintings. So I'll leave you and John for a moment, while I direct them to the work we need to do."

Agatha led her team into the living room and then through the dining room, and, as Doreen watched, Agatha pointed out which paintings she was taking.

John looked at her quizzically. "I guess this is quite chaotic for you, isn't it?"

Doreen chuckled. "Chaotic, wonderful, scary, all of the above," she admitted. "You don't realize how valuable something is until somebody tells you, and then you look at it with completely different eyes, and you're worried you did something earlier to damage it."

He nodded. "Maybe you could show me the books, and I could be the first one to be done."

She gave him a wide smile. "Come on," she said. "We're in the quiet corner of the house."

She led the way through to the kitchen and then to the alcove where she kept the printer, next to the pantry. "So this is the area of junk," she said with a half a grin. "And I hadn't realized the books stored here in the pantry were worth anything. I had my nan over, who is responsible for all the purchases in this house, and she pulled out the ones she thought were the most valuable and stacked them here." She turned and pointed to a few books on the chair at the edge of the table. "So maybe start with those."

"Good," he said, "it sounds like she has already done half the work for me."

Doreen pulled out a second chair before motioning to an empty one and said, "If you would like to sit, enjoy."

He sat down, looked at the cup of coffee in her hand, and asked, "Is that coffee?"

She chuckled. "I usually put a pot on when I know Scott's coming," she said. "Would you like a cup?"

"I would love a cup," he said warmly, "and thank you very much for being such a lovely hostess." Then he picked up the first book, and he was lost.

She stood for a moment as she watched his rapt face while turning the pages, gently looking at copyrights, condition, bindings. More unnerved than she expected to be, she poured the last of the old coffee into a cup and made a fresh pot. She knew Scott would drink at least one of the cups, and she suspected this pot would be gone quickly too.

When she had it dripping, she sat down beside John and waited for him to speak. He'd set two books on the table side by side. She didn't know if that was the start of his piles or if that was just because he wanted to keep the books separated. She didn't ask any questions, just waited quietly. Then she remembered the music. She went to the corner of the pantry, jam-packed full of paperwork, so much so that she hadn't had a chance to go through it all. Maybe while John was looking at the books was a good time.

She grabbed a couple stacks, making one huge stack, which completely emptied that shelf. Doreen brought everything to the kitchen table, sat down at one end, and sorted, making piles on the floor and piles on the remaining chairs.

She had a Recipes stack; she had Notes from Nan about various things that Doreen would have to ask her about, like these information articles. Apparently Nan was curious about *everything*. Doreen sorted through piece after piece until she had a big stack that made no sense to her, so she would be forced to ask Nan about all this. She further sorted this big stack into informational pieces Nan had printed off, articles she'd torn out of magazines and newspapers, pamphlets she'd been given, even take-out menus. Once done, Doreen was up and gathering another stack.

She was on the fourth pantry shelf holding just assorted pages of paper and feeling damn good about what was happening when John made an odd sound. She looked at him and asked in a quiet voice, "Are you okay?"

He held up the *Ulysses* book. "This is a first printing," he said. "First edition, first printing." He turned to look at her, his gaze wide. "Do you have any idea what it's worth?"

She shook her head. "I have no clue. I'm so far out of the realm of what any of this is worth that every price is shocking me."

He said, "It's …" He was at a loss for words. "… priceless?" At that, he gave a soft chuckle, breaking his reverie. "Well, there will be collectors who want to pay a price for it. And I hesitate to even suggest what it could be worth. It will be in a prime spot in the Christie's catalog though. If it even makes it that far. I do have a number of private collectors. I'll have to see what kind of price they're willing to pay."

"Is that fair?" she asked curiously. "At least in the catalog, everybody gets a chance to bid."

"Spoken like a true entrepreneur," he said. "Because, in the catalog, of course, the bidding could go much higher than any estimate."

"Well, I have no clue," she said. "So you are the professional, and you need to tell me the best way forward."

He still held *Ulysses* in his hand with such a reverence that she realized just how wrong it was for her to own these pieces. "You're just reinforcing that I need to sell these books," she said quietly. "You have such a reverence for them, such a respect, and, for me, they're just dusty old tomes."

At that, he looked shocked, and then he spluttered with laughter. "At least you're honest, my dear."

"I am, at that," she said, "and I'm still stuck at the stage where money is food, and I'm in survival mode," she admitted. "But, even if I had lots of money, this wouldn't be my choice of what to spend it on. They just don't appeal to me. Part of me feels bad because these are very special items, but I'm just not the rightful owner."

"There are people who would be very glad to hear that," he said, "because they do want to be the rightful owners."

She motioned at the books in front of him. "You have four there. Are any of them decent or just the one in your hand?"

"All of them are valuable," he admitted, his fingers gently stroking the leather bindings on the surface of each of the four. "Very different categories, different prices, but, if you agree, I'll take all four."

She nodded and smiled. "And that stack?"

He smiled gently. "Don't rush me," he said. "When it's a thing of beauty, you want to take the right time to honor it."

And he returned to the *Ulysses* book in his hand, his fingers almost trembling.

She sighed happily. "Nan will be delighted to know she made such good investments."

He smiled at her and said, "Your nan is a genius."

"In many, many ways," Doreen said. "She had a lot of fun doing this."

"Then she's lucky too," John said. "Because too often, collectors become obsessive over their finds, where she appears to have not even taken care of them properly."

Doreen felt horrified at that comment. But then as she looked at the stack of books and the shelves they were on, she had to admit he had a point. "For her, I think it was the joy of the find, the hunt, the negotiating. It wasn't about acquiring. It wasn't about ownership. It was about the joy of the process."

"Some people are like that," he said. "You're very blessed."

He reached for the next book. She watched him for a moment and then gave herself a shake. The moving men were here—she needed to find as much as she could while they were still going through this stuff. She got up and removed everything from the next two shelves in the pantry so she had a big stack in front of her on the kitchen table. She still had a couple shorter shelves on one side and more across from that, all filled with paper. She needed to speed this up if she had any hope of getting through this before the experts left.

Focused, she quickly sorted and tossed some into her Trash pile, making sure not one of those pieces of paper was of any value or at least any value at first glance. She'd have to go through it one more time later before actually tossing this pile. The pile of Unknowns was a bit of a curiosity too, but it was the smallest of the piles.

An hour later she sat back. She refilled everyone's coffee and returned to the two short shelves in the pantry. She removed everything from those two shelves, stacking it up on the kitchen table, and went through it all. When she turned around next, Scott smiled at her stacks of paperwork and said, "At least you're getting through some of this now."

She nodded. "Those two shelving units in the pantry there, the standalone cherry ones, let me know if they're of any interest to you or whether I can fully reload them again," she said with a laugh.

He examined them both and said, "Just go ahead and refill them, but maybe with a little bit more care."

She nodded. "I will do that." She had stacks everywhere, but one of the biggest piles was designated as Garbage/Trash. She grabbed a large brown paper grocery bag, found she needed two of them, and filled them both full of stuff she wasn't keeping.

With some of that cleaned up, and three good stacks on the table now, she went back to another bookshelf in the pantry. She started with the little one this time, where she had moved recipe books to the far side and then realized the front closet had more recipe books too. She removed the items as fast as she could until the small shelving unit was empty; then she began in on the bigger shelving unit again. By the time she'd emptied the top two shelves, the table was stacked full of stuff again.

She groaned. Working as fast as she could, she sorted piece of paper after piece of paper. If she couldn't tell what it was, she stuck it in the Ask Nan pile. It took an hour before she could finally lift her head, and John stared at her in amazement.

She glanced at him and smiled. "Lots of this stuff is just

junk," she said, motioning to the pile on the floor. "Some of it, as you can see, is a collection of take-out menus which, by now, are so old and outdated they might as well go in the garbage too. That's the Ask Nan pile. Here are all the recipes Nan has printed off, and this is paperwork of some kind I still have to sort through."

He nodded and said, "It's a really good thing you're doing this then."

She smiled. "Indeed, it is." She glanced at his stack. She'd kept her eye on it the whole time she'd worked, and he still had three books to go. Instead of stacked up, the books were now stretched out across his end of the kitchen table beside each other. "Any luck?"

"Phenomenal luck," he said. "So far I'll take every one off your hands."

She beamed. "This sounds like a very lucky day for me. I know more things of value could be in here, and I just want to make sure I have a chance to search through everything while you guys are here." She took the stuff off of the third and fourth shelves, stacked it up, and then dropped to her knees and pulled out the cookbooks and other books on the bottom shelf. "You let me know if anything here has any value," she said as she laid them out one at a time atop her end of the kitchen table.

He looked at them and said, "Cookbooks? I highly doubt it."

She said, "This one's turn-of-the-century, I think, but I don't know which century." He held out a hand, and she handed it to him. The others were much more modern, so she moved them to the other pantry shelf. "Now look at that. I have two empty sets of shelving and a big mess in the kitchen," she said with a chuckle.

"This cookbook is valuable," he said. "Certainly not on the same level as all these other books but definitely a few thousand dollars."

She looked at it, smiled, and said, "Perfect. Then that one's for you too."

Chapter 18

Tuesday Noon ...

D OREEN WENT BACK to sorting, her mind and heart alight with joy. Yet she could feel everything rolling in her stomach and a certain quarreling through her system, a tension, worried something might still go wrong before the experts took things into their possession. As she went through Nan's papers, a couple letters she added to the Ask Nan pile. Most of this last stack was junk, which Nan had printed off on various different medical conditions which didn't pertain to anything at this point—not Doreen's cold cases, not Nan's own health. Lots of the Garbage pile was just pamphlets, religious pamphlets, like collecting anything that came in the mail too. Or maybe just not going through her mail every day. Doreen could see that. After a while, it would have accumulated, and Nan would have taken her growing pile of mail and then finally shoved it on the shelf. So she could go through it later. *Later, right.* By the time Doreen got to that, she was tired. She sat down with a heavy *thump* and said, "Well, those shelves full of papers are done."

John smiled, looked at the stack on the floor, and whistled. "So most of it was garbage?"

She nodded as she swept up the stack of take-out menus off the table and dumped them on the floor into her Trash pile. "Most of it was garbage. This stack is Recipes," she said. "I'll put them on the cookbook shelf. This is my Ask Nan pile, stuff for Nan to go through, if she cares, and stuff I have questions about, with two letters I found on the top." She picked them up and said, "These letters are dated quite a while ago. I don't know what they are."

She handed them to John and snagged the stack of recipes, moved them to the pantry shelf designated for them now, where they could stand between two larger recipe books and then stared at the one wall of empty shelves with pride. She left the pantry for the small nearby alcove. "Now for the hutch under the printer," she said to herself as she dropped down, opened up the base of the hutch, and pulled out the big folders in there.

She had no clue if any of this was valuable, but Scott was taking the hutch, and that would happen sooner rather than later. Considering the movers had already taken so many other pieces, she was surprised Scott hadn't come in after the hutch yet. It also meant the printer would have to sit on the floor, unless maybe a kitchen chair could hold it. She took a chair and moved the printer onto it and then emptied the inside and the top of the hutch. With everything back on the kitchen table, she groaned and said, "Man, she was a collector."

Just then Scott walked in, took one look at the hutch, and crowed, "I was hoping you'd get to that."

She smiled and said, "Go ahead and take it. I still have no place to put some of this stuff, but it's empty."

He looked at it in admiration. "Looks like you've done a tremendous amount of clearing out. Anything valuable?"

"An old English cookbook," she said. "I'm not sure about the rest of this stuff yet, and I just got into the contents of the hutch. I did all the bookshelves full of paper in the pantry first."

Scott disappeared, then returned with two men. They carefully picked up the hutch and moved it into the living room.

She looked at John, who was staring at the letters. "Do you know anything about them?" she said. "You're looking at them like they're important."

"They are important, I think," John said, frowning, "but I'm not sure. They could be really good fakes."

"They could be," she said. "I have no idea."

Scott looked at her newest stacks on the kitchen table and asked, "What's all that? It's very different from the rest of the stuff you took off the shelves."

"This was all in the hutch," she said to John. "Do you know anything about music?"

He pulled his spectacles off his nose, and she opened up the leather folder to show sheets of music. He held out his hand and asked, "May I?"

She handed it to him. "I think each of these is from a different musician, but I don't know. Nan tried to explain some of it to me, but it was a little confusing."

John carefully removed all the sheet music from the folder in front of him and said, "Musician notes are here too." He read through some of it, flipping through the pages, and said, "I'm not a musician, but these all appear to be the unpublished works of somebody. I just don't know who this is."

"I don't either," Doreen said, "and I don't even know if the music is any good." Just then she caught sight of a piece of paper sticking out from inside the folder. She motioned to it and pulled it out. "Oh, look at that. It's a bill of sale."

He opened it up and together they read it. "Interesting," he said. "This isn't my field, but I do know somebody interested in this type of stuff."

She burst out laughing at that. "It's like you expert guys all know each other."

"When you think about it," he said, "we all work for Christie's, so we get to know each other in our various fields." He looked at the three other matching envelopes. "Are those leather folders also holding music?"

"I'm not sure," she said. She opened the second one and nodded. "And another bill of sale. Before you take any of this," she said, "I want to scan all the music so I have a copy of it. I have no clue what this is, so I hate to see it leave my possession without knowing."

"I'll take a couple photos of the notes and some of the music," John said, "and I'll send it to the music expert I know." He was already taking photos of various sheets. "I'll leave it in your possession unless it proves valuable."

"Good enough," she said. She went through the next two folders. "All four of these contain music." She found a place on a pantry bookshelf near the bottom where she could stack the folders. "When you're done, we'll put them all there."

He nodded and said, "That's a good place to keep them for the moment."

With those out of the way, she went back to the rest of the stuff. She opened a small box and found something like a paperweight in a small clear box. She held it out for John. "Does this mean anything to you?"

He frowned and shook his head.

"I'll ask Agatha," Doreen said. She walked through the dining room, realizing the paintings were already gone. In the living room, everything was pretty well gone, just the two chairs she wasn't sure if Scott was taking or not. She headed out to the garage, almost crowing in delight to see it so empty. The men had the back of the moving truck wide open, and it was packed nearly full. She shook her head.

Scott saw her and walked toward her. "Hard to believe all this came out of the house, isn't it?"

"I'm stunned. I'm really stunned." She held up the see-through box with the paperweight in it. "Do you know anything about this?"

He frowned. "Nope, doesn't mean anything to me. What about Agatha?" Turning around, Scott pointed down the driveway. "She's down there. They packed up several of the paintings, and they're putting them in her transport vehicle now." It was a panel van, and Doreen walked down to it.

Agatha saw her coming, smiled, and said, "We've got two more to pack up, and then we're good."

"Wonderful," Doreen said. She held out the object in her palm. "Do you know what this is?"

Agatha reached out a hand and studied it carefully. "There's a piece of paper behind it." Using her nails she pulled it out without having to remove the object from the box. "It's a piece of rare crystal, hand-carved by a glass worker out of Venice." She frowned, carefully removed the crystal from the clear box, and held it up to the sunlight as a million colors exploded from the crystal. Everybody gasped.

"It's beautiful," Doreen said.

"Not only is it beautiful, it's been kept in pristine condition," Agatha said. "This bill of sale and declaration of authenticity says Italy 1842."

Doreen just shook her head. "I have no idea where Nan got all this stuff."

Agatha looked at it with a happy sigh, carefully replacing the paper in the clear box. "What would you like to do with this?"

"What are my choices?" Doreen asked drily. "I already have nightmares how the house is full of things that I don't know are valuable and either give those away or lose or break the rest."

Agatha said, "I'd be happy to take this. I might have to do a bit more research to figure out its value, but I think it's certainly a lovely piece, and I'm sure it will sell."

"Good," Doreen said. "Take it." And she laughed. "Between all of you, I won't have much left in my house."

"No," one of the men beside Agatha said, "you may not. On the other hand, your bank account will be very full."

At that, the truth really sank in. "You're right," she said quietly. "And, for that, I'm desperately thankful. It's been a very long year, and I can't begin to express how much I appreciate you guys doing this."

"Hey, it's business," Agatha said warmly. "But these pieces go well beyond business. Collectors all over the world will stand in line to touch and to hold some of these. So you should feel good about that too. I have paperwork for you as well, once we get the other two paintings loaded. We'll go over every one of the items that I'm taking today, and I'll give you a receipt for them."

"Did you go through the whole house?" Doreen asked.

"I thought so," Agatha said. "But, if you have a few moments, maybe we can take another look."

"My grandmother did say something about a painting in

one of the closets, and I haven't found it yet," Doreen said sadly. "Something about a woman in black sitting on the edge of a chair. She said it was very ugly but thought it was worth a lot of money."

Agatha chuckled. "If it's the one I know about, she's right. It's worth a ton of money."

Doreen nodded. "Why don't we go up and take a look? If we search every room carefully, we might find it."

"Then let's go. I haven't been in the basement either," Agatha said. "I've seen them bring piece after piece out of there, but I have yet to have a look myself."

"Let's start there," Doreen said. "If you have any interest in old kitchen stuff, that's probably the best place to go." Just then her phone beeped. Mack sending her info on Crystal's case. Torn, she wanted to go inside and study what he'd sent, then caught sight of Agatha's curious gaze. She smiled, pocketed her phone, and said, "Let's do another check of the house."

Chapter 19

Tuesday Afternoon ...

THEY STARTED IN the garage, and Doreen cried out, "When Scott arrived yesterday morning, this garage was stuffed!"

"Hard to believe," Agatha said. "It's almost as if your grandmother had a furniture warehouse instead of a home."

Doreen led the way downstairs to the basement, crying out in joy again. "And look at this," she said. "This was stuffed floor-to-ceiling. We moved a ton up into the garage, but it was still full down here. Now it's almost empty!"

"It's hard to believe this storage area is here. Those stairs make a massive difference."

"True. It did eat into some of the space though," Doreen said as she walked around the corner beside the stairs. "And this is the first time that I realized a door was here. This area was full of chairs." She clicked on the light overhead and then opened the door. "Looks like I found them."

Together they pulled out what appeared to be six large picture frames. It was hard to move them, but it would have been impossible before with all the furniture here. They laid them out and stacked them up against the wall so they could all be seen easily. While Agatha studied them, Doreen crawled into this closet under the stairs to make sure it was empty. She used her cell phone, turned on the flashlight, and checked out every corner. Satisfied it was a hundred percent empty, she stepped out, closed the door, turned to look at Agatha, and heard more good news. Agatha held her hands clasped to her chest, and Doreen knew what a massive gift her nan was.

She sent Nan a text saying, **If I haven't said so in a while, I just want to tell you that I love you.** When a text came back with several hearts in a row, she smiled and answered, **The appraisers are here. We just found the painting you told me about and more under the stairs in the basement.**

Nan replied with **Oh, good. I forgot about those.**

Doreen texted her back saying, **Any idea what else you've forgotten? LOL.**

Nan's response was instant. **Nope. The good news is, you're finding it all. And that makes me even happier. They're all for you, so enjoy.**

As Doreen put away her phone, she looked at Agatha, who still hadn't moved. Doreen asked calmly, "I gather this is good news?"

Agatha turned, looked at her, and smiled. "For you, very good news."

Then Doreen realized she had something else to consider, another motive behind kidnapping Crystal. What if Crystal had seen something she wasn't supposed to see?

Chapter 20

Tuesday Late Afternoon ...

B Y THE TIME her house emptied of people once again, Doreen felt like a limp dishrag that had been pulled out of the dryer too soon. Instead of being light and fluffy and ready to go again, she felt like she needed more time in the dryer because she wasn't quite there yet. She collapsed on a pot chair in the living room and stared at her now unbelievably empty house. Pictures were gone from the walls, at least the ones of any value. She could only see one left, and that was in the hallway. She had the two pot chairs; she had Thaddeus's roost still in the living room, and she had an old busted-up coffee table that had been downstairs in the basement.

Probably more junk was supposed to come up and didn't quite get to the garage. It would work for the moment though. She was too tired to even get up and fix a cup of tea, and that said a lot about her state. Thaddeus hopped onto her shoulder and gently rubbed his head against her cheek. She was almost teary-eyed as she reached up to cuddle him. "I hope this is all worth it," she whispered.

He made an odd crooning sound in the back of his

throat that put a smile on her face.

"Well, just think about it. If it does work, there'll be birdseed for you until you die." And then she corrected that, "Depending on how long you live, that is."

She dropped her head onto the back of the pot chair and winced because it was just a little too low for comfort. She would have to slide her butt to the edge of the seat in order to make her head comfortable. She was afraid she would slide right off. Mugs jumped onto her lap. "Great. Thanks, Mugs. At least your weight holds me in place," she said in exhaustion. And then she felt another *thump*, and, sure enough, Goliath jumped onto the back of the chair and patted her shoulder to brush his head against her head too. She groaned. "Thanks, guys. I just needed a few minutes to recuperate."

After that, she'd walk around to see what was left. The stack of transfer papers, documenting her items relegated to Christie's, which she had been diligent in marking off with each and every expert as they removed items, was on the kitchen table. She understood it would be months and months and months before any of this came to a successful conclusion, and all of it wouldn't happen at once, but this was an incredible journey, and she had so much to thank Nan for that again, tears came to the corner of her eyes.

She brushed away the tears and said, "I shouldn't be crying. I should be thanking her." But she wasn't up for conversation either. She was just too damn tired. She groaned again, but this time it was more of a release of the breath in her chest as she sagged even deeper into this incredibly uncomfortable position. The floor would be better. At least that way she'd be flat on the ground. She stayed like this in the chair, unwilling to move yet, no matter how uncomfortable, and her eyes closed for several long moments until she lost track of time. Her ringing phone brought her out of her weird dozing state. She saw Nan's name and hit Talk. "Hello, Nan."

"Oh my, you don't sound very good," Nan said, her tone worried. "Are you okay? Do you need an ambulance? What's the matter?"

At that, Doreen realized how bad she sounded. She pulled herself together and said, "No, no, I'm fine. Don't worry about me. Everybody finally left the house, and I'm just sitting here, exhausted."

"You have every right to be, my dear," Nan said. "I mean, just think. It took me years and years and years, actually decades and decades and decades," she corrected, "to collect all that. And here you've disposed of it all within a few days."

Doreen was oddly silent, then said slowly, "Somehow that makes me feel even worse."

Nan burst out into rich laughter that rolled through the phone. "Oh my, don't at all. I had incredible amounts of fun collecting and trading up for all that stuff. But, for you, it was just dusty old pieces, cluttering up your life, so the best thing you could have done is get rid of it all."

"Especially when you said so many of these pieces were *ugly*," Doreen said with emphasis. "And I have to agree with you. So many of them were so ugly."

Nan chuckled. "They were worth a lot though," she said. "What you need is a good cup of tea."

"I was thinking that," Doreen said, "but honestly, I'm too tired to walk to the kitchen to make it."

"Get up," Nan said firmly. "Grab the animals and come here. The walk will invigorate you, even if it takes twice the time because you're dragging your feet. I'll have a nice little treat waiting and a hot cup of tea." And then she hung up, not giving Doreen a chance to argue. Doreen stared at her phone, let it collapse on her belly, and heaved out the heaviest sigh she'd ever exhaled in her life. When she opened her eyes after that, all three animals stared at her, the worry clearly evident in their expressions. She'd never seen Mugs's eyes so round, and Thaddeus had pitched that gimlet look on his face, as if daring her to die on him. She stroked Goliath's ears as he tilted his head at her. "I'm fine guys, honest. I'm okay."

Reassured by her voice, the animals visibly relaxed, and she realized just how worried they'd been. She sat up slowly, carefully moving Mugs to the floor, and said, "Well, it looks like we're going for a walk, whether we want to or not." She headed out the front door and realized for the first time there was no point in setting the alarm. But it was a habit now, and she still had a lot of stuff to take down to Wendy, and a few things remained on the mantel, but she had no idea what was left. She needed to do a full assessment, but that wasn't today's job. That would have to wait until tomorrow. She figured Wednesday was a good day for catching up.

Today she was too exhausted to do anything else but visit Nan. If she was lucky, the treat was big enough to be dinner, and then she would sit out by the creek with a book and ignore life for the rest of the evening. Hopefully tomorrow, with a good night's sleep, she'd feel better. Nan was right, it did take twice the time to get to her place. But somehow, walking along the creek, even slowly, did revitalize Doreen's soul. She stopped and smiled at the antics of the ducks, wandering up and down the creek in the sun as it dappled against the trees.

It had been a very early spring this year, and she didn't know when the flooding would come, but the river was rising rapidly. It was a little worrisome, but it hadn't been a terribly bad winter—at least she didn't think so—so it shouldn't be a bad flood season. Yet, in this area, it was something she would keep an eye on.

Little Paul was never far from her mind when she thought about Kelowna's flood season. To think that little boy and the kind man had lost their lives in that turbulent water. Not that she liked the creek any less, it was just one of those reminders about making sure she didn't take the creek and the mild weather for granted and didn't discount the ferocity of Mother Nature when she was at her strongest.

Finally, with great joy Doreen turned the corner and saw the retirement building looming ahead. She walked past the front entrance and, using the stepping stones Nan had placed there for her, she walked over to the little border of garden beds and stepped onto Nan's patio.

Nan came out of the apartment with her arms open. "Oh, my dear, you look so exhausted."

Doreen bent down, gave her a hug, and said, "Honestly, I am. I didn't think selling all that furniture and stuff would take so much out of me. And I'm still stressed, thinking that maybe I missed something."

Nan chuckled. "If you did, I'm sure they will come back. It's all very good stuff."

Doreen sat down with a heavy *thump*. "You realize what a gold mine you've given me, right?"

Nan nodded. "When I started this originally, I didn't really plan on all of it," she said. "I was thinking of you as soon as you were born because I didn't want you to want for anything. Don't take this the wrong way, dearie, but your mother is not exactly somebody I could trust with funds."

"That's an understatement," Doreen muttered. Her mother had been a lot of things, but frugal was not one of them. "So you figured, if you put the money in investments, like antiques instead of gold and/or stocks, then they would still be around. It was risky though," Doreen added. "Because, if you think about it, that house could have caught fire, and all of it would have gone up in smoke." At that, she gave herself a mental shake and said, "And I really didn't need to voice that fear because now I'll have nightmares about it."

Nan patted her hand gently and said, "But you did find the right people and moved it all safely."

Doreen just smiled at her, loving the birdlike woman in front of her. "You're such a blessing in my life," she whispered. Feeling the tears once again coming to the corners of her eyes, she impatiently brushed them away.

When she opened them again, a massive still-warm meat pie sat in front of her. She looked at it in amazement. "This looks wonderful," she said, sniffing the heavy and rich aroma. "And smells even better."

Nan nodded. "It does, doesn't it? We had these at lunch today. I picked one up for you. I'm still worried you're not getting enough to eat."

Doreen laughed. "Anytime Mack comes over, he feeds me," she admitted. "Although, when he came to collect my intruder, there was no time for food."

"Another intruder. Oh dear." Nan picked up a fork, handed it to her, and said, "Dig in. It's a lovely lamb pie." Doreen used the fork and cut into the crust, releasing the hot steam inside. "This is a perfect end to a really long day." And she slowly ate.

While she did, Nan chatted on about everybody in the Rosemoor facility. From Mitzi and her boyfriend, who was Nan's ex-boyfriend, splitting up, to the manager Nan had gotten into trouble with for betting on his love life and later on having a new girlfriend. When she heard that, Doreen asked in warning, "You didn't start a pool on his love life, did you?"

Nan looked at her with a bland smile. "You know what? If they weren't such fun and got themselves into all this drama, we wouldn't have to do it."

Doreen rolled her eyes. "Tell yourself whatever excuses you want," she said, "but you know it's wrong." She picked up another bite of the pie and sat back, enjoying her meal thoroughly. When there was a soft gentle *woof* beside her, she looked down to see Mugs staring up at her with the most woebegone look she could imagine.

She hesitated, and Nan jumped to her feet. "No, no, no, I have something for him too." She walked back inside to her little kitchenette. When she returned, she carried tiny sausages. "I figured these would be good for him." She bent down, breaking chunks off the sausage for Mugs. Happily, Mugs devoured every piece as it came his way, but Goliath was quick to have his nose in a joint. He hopped up into Nan's lap without warning, causing her to cry out in surprise, but Nan wrapped her arms around the huge Maine coon cat and hugged him close. "Oh, I do miss these guys," she said.

"That may be," Doreen said, "but do you have any treats for him too?"

Nan beamed. "I do." And out of her pocket she pulled some little triangles. "These are some fancy new thing I saw at the pet store," she said, and she placed one on the corner of the table. Goliath very gently stood up on his back legs and bent down, picking up the kernel in his mouth and crunching away quite happily.

Between the sausages for Mugs and the treats for Goliath, those two were happy, but Thaddeus had no intention of being left out. He paced around the table, raising and lowering his head, ruffling his feathers, looking at Nan, reminding her, "Thaddeus is here. Thaddeus is here."

Nan chuckled. "How could I forget you?" And out of her other pocket she pulled several sunflower seeds. She put them on the table in front of him.

Doreen watched as everybody ate, including herself, and she smiled at Nan. "See what I mean?" Doreen asked. "You're such a godsend in my life."

"Not anywhere near as much as you are in mine," Nan said firmly. "Now, are you ready to get down to business?"

Chapter 21

Tuesday Early Evening ...

D OREEN'S HEAD SNAPPED up as she stared at Nan. "What kind of business?"

"Crystal's father has a criminal record," Nan said.

"Crystal's father has a criminal record?" Doreen repeated slowly. "Seriously? For what?"

"Buying and selling illegal goods," Nan said in a low whisper, looking around as if somebody would hear them.

Unable to help herself, Doreen also looked around, but, of course, they were surrounded by Mother Nature and not much else. "How do you know this?"

"José, one of the attendants here. His brother used to work for Crystal's father."

Doreen pinched her nose as she thought about the connections inside Rosemoor, the vast knowledge and network of both staff and residents—or *inmates* as Nan lovingly referred to them.

"And how does that relate to Crystal's disappearance?"

"José has a theory, but he hasn't said much. He muttered something about Eric and blackmailing, even mentioned his sister, but was not clear on any of it." Nan continued, "Of course I don't know if José knows anything useful or if he's just spouting conspiracy theories."

Slowly Doreen lowered her fork. "And how did José know Crystal's father was a blackmailer?" she asked. "Did he go to the police about it?"

Nan twittered. "Oh, no. He knew because Eric was blackmailing him and his brother."

Dumbfounded, Doreen just stared at her grandmother, her mind spinning, as she thought about how many more people had a reason to get back at Crystal's father. "But why take the child? As revenge? Or was this a kidnapping, with ransom demanded? But then where is Crystal? Or was this a kidnapping gone wrong?"

"You'll have to ask Mack about that," Nan said. "But it's possible. Although I don't remember ever hearing anything about a ransom demand."

"What it does is widen the suspect pool though," Doreen said slowly. "And that's both good and bad."

"What's bad about it?" Nan asked curiously. "Now you have more suspects to look at."

"Yes, but that's too many more," she said. "Because now I have to investigate José and his brother, along with Eric, and where does the new stepmom come into play?"

At that, Nan chuckled. "Mary is José and Guido's sister."

Bingo. Now they were getting somewhere. "Good Lord," Doreen said, sitting back.

Nan, completely nonplussed at the bombshell she had just dropped, picked up the pot of tea and filled Doreen's cup. "Eat up. Eat up," she urged.

Doreen picked up her fork again and finished the meat pie while she thought about the criminal games adults played and the young girl caught in the middle. "Does José have any theories on what happened to the little girl?" she asked.

Nan lowered her voice yet again. "He says he thinks she's still alive."

At that, Doreen's gaze flew up to study Nan's face, her eyes alight with excitement.

"If she's alive, where is she?" Doreen asked. "It would be really nice to find somebody alive this time instead of another mess of dead bones."

"Wouldn't it?" Nan said, chuckling. "But José had no clue where."

"He must have some idea," she said. "If he's come up with that idea, he must have a thought process that led him to it."

"Maybe," Nan said, "but he's not very forthcoming."

"Of course not. However, maybe over time, in little bits and nudges …" she suggested.

Nan bobbed her head. "My thoughts exactly," she said.

"Do you know where Guido works?"

"He owns his own pawn shop now," Nan said. "But José got training so he could work as a service care aide."

"But he used to work with his brother?" Doreen clarified. "I have to know who and what I'm dealing with because it certainly defines whether we can trust the information he's offering."

"He didn't ask for money for the information," Nan said. "But it's possible he might accept some in return for more information."

It went against everything Doreen believed in, but, if a little girl-teenager-now was out there alive, she needed to be returned to her family—if they were trustworthy people. And what was that worth? For Doreen it was priceless, but she didn't have much money. "Does he need money?" she asked.

"Absolutely," Nan said. "He's got four kids, and his wife just lost her job because she's going onto medical disability. She's got really severe fibromyalgia."

"I'm not sure what that is," Doreen said, "but I don't have any money to pay him."

"No, no, no, no, of course you don't," Nan said. "I didn't mean that at all."

"Maybe not," Doreen said, "but I have to see if there is more information. Of course he doesn't want to talk to Mack, does he?"

"Nope, not at all."

"And, before I paid for any information," Doreen said, her mind spinning on all of the things that could come out of something from an informant like that, "we'd need proof of life."

Nan clapped her hands together in delight. "Oh my, you sound so efficient."

Doreen flushed, placed her fork on the plate, then moved it slightly away. Mugs made a slight *woof.* She looked down at him, removed the fork from her plate, and held the plate for him to lick up all the rich gravy. "It's not that I'm officially investigating this matter in any capacity," she reminded Nan. "That's something I have to remember. But there is always detective jargon left in my brain after I read all these related articles that I find on the internet."

"Of course you are reading tons of articles." Nan studied Doreen. "Aren't you?"

Doreen nodded. "Yes," she said. "But there is only so much we can find online. Somehow I have to loosen the tongues of those with dark secrets who need to tell someone.

It's like the secret eats away at their souls until they can share it. If they've done something wrong, they often want their actions validated or to boast of their actions."

"That's why solving cold cases works so well for you," Nan said, "because, over time, some of these people are facing their own mortality and need to clear the air."

"True," Doreen said. "But sometimes people are also doing it for other reasons. Sometimes they think it doesn't matter. Sometimes they think it's way too late to be punished. People have all kinds of reasons for doing things like that."

Doreen picked the plate up from Mugs, put it on the table, and said, "Let me do some research on the family, particularly the stepmom. I know Clara was very suspicious of Mary."

"But that's almost a given, isn't it?" Nan asked. "Nobody likes to have the replacement wife looking after your child."

At that, Doreen winced. "I was replaced, but thankfully I didn't have a child in the middle." And, for the first time, she thought about what a blessing it was that she hadn't had children yet.

She couldn't imagine joint custody and then realized sadly her husband would never have let her have even that much. Money did buy a lot of things in life, and, in this case, it would have bought a child's custody away from her. She sat back with her tea, sipped it, and said, "You've certainly given me some interesting things to think about."

"What do you think it means?" Nan asked, leaning forward. "I do respect your brain, dear."

Doreen chuckled. "You might," she said, "but not too many other people do." She thought about this new information. "I guess you don't have a photo of this José, Guido, or Mary, do you?"

Nan shook her head. "Nope, I don't. And José isn't working today. I was hoping he could talk to you while you were here."

"He won't want to talk to me," Doreen said. "At least I don't think so." She opened her purse, pulled out a little notebook, ripped off a piece of paper, and wrote down her cell phone number. "But, if he does, have him call me."

Nan grabbed the piece of paper, folded it, and tucked it in her pocket. "He's due back here tomorrow morning," she said. "You never know what you might find out."

"No," Doreen said, "I don't." Her mind was now consumed with the problem and a kernel of an idea that wouldn't let go. But it was just a working theory. She didn't have any proof, and she needed to do a lot more research first.

"That's an interesting look on your face," Nan said in excitement. "You have a theory, don't you?"

"I have a theory," Doreen said, "but nothing to say it's right. There has been a lot of theories for ten years. But that means nothing."

"You don't think she's dead, do you?" Nan asked.

"I never thought she was dead," Doreen said after a moment's reflection. "But that's just an instinctive answer. There's no real way to know why or how. We have to find her before anybody will know the truth."

"She'd be eighteen by now, and who knows what she looks like," Nan said. "Maybe you can get Mack to do one of those age-progression things."

Doreen chuckled. "Maybe, and most likely not. You let me worry about that." She pushed her chair back and looked down at the animals. "Are you guys ready to go home?"

Apologetically she said to Nan, "We're pretty tired, and I still have to walk ten to fifteen minutes to get home." She stopped for a moment. "Do you have any idea where José and Guido live?"

"The pawn shop is up in the Rutland area of town, but I think Guido lives in the Glenmore area. Jose lives close by."

Doreen vaguely knew those areas. Kelowna had once been a bunch of small communities that grew into each other before becoming Kelowna itself, but it was still full of small community names of the original settlements. "Okay, that's not terribly helpful," she said, "but I'll think about it."

With that she gave Nan a big hug and a kiss. "Thank you so much for dinner. It was wonderful." Seeing she'd been here an hour and a half, she slowly took her leave and headed toward the creek again. With a happy and full tummy, a lovely cup of tea, sharing some memories, and now new information to puzzle on, she strolled home. Halfway there, her phone rang. "Hey, Mack," she said. "What's up?"

"Nothing in particular, but my instincts kept saying you were heading into or already in trouble."

"What do you mean *already?*" she cried in outrage. "I haven't been in trouble all day."

"Did Scott finish?"

"Scott, Agatha, and John," she said, the fatigue once again taking over her voice. "It's been a hell of a day. I just had dinner at Nan's and got spoon-fed some very interesting new information on Crystal's case. Now I'm walking home."

"What kind of new information?" Mack asked, his voice turning official.

"Probably nothing," she said airily.

"Doreen ..." he said, his voice heavy and hard. "It's still

an open case for us."

"I'm thinking the child's alive still," she said, giving him part of the information.

There was silence on the other end, and then Mack said, "Do you have anything to back that up?"

"Maybe," she said.

His voice was emotional this time. "I'd do a lot to bring that child home. It's one of the cases that's weighed on me all these years."

"Then you'll be happy if I bring her home." And very gently, she hung up on him.

Chapter 22

Tuesday Evening...

DOREEN REALLY HAD to stop hanging up on Mack like that. His voice carried a load of hurt, something she needed to explore a little deeper.

Ten years ago he would have been a cop, and so he'd been involved in Crystal's kidnapping case. Maybe he'd known the people involved personally. Regardless of how his involvement came about, it was obvious this case caused him pain. And the fact that there'd been another footprint, which made no sense, was a prod that could only remind him of Crystal's absence. He would want to be kept up-to-date with anything she could find.

The problem was, so far, it was just theories based on hearsay, and theories and hearsay wouldn't do anybody any good—especially to an officer of the law. And driving around Rutland or the Glenmore area wouldn't help if she couldn't get specific addresses. She'd need Mack's help with that. And, even with addresses, all she could do was drive by their houses. She needed more information. The fact that it came all the way back to Mary's involvement with Eric meant somehow they were behind all this.

If Mary had wanted to get rid of Crystal, it would have been easy enough to have enlisted her brothers' help. While both might have been eager to help, one might have helped, but the other one might have wanted something for his part in this. But getting Mary to confess would be next to impossible. Ten years had gone by, ten years where she'd gotten away scot-free, where she had benefited, either from not being punished because of her part in this kidnapping or just to be rid of Crystal and to not share Eric with his daughter.

And maybe this was all a plot by the brothers to get back at Eric for blackmailing them. And then again, maybe Eric was dealing with a lot of bad customers in his illegal buying-and-selling business, and things had gone very wrong. Doreen had no doubt that, of Crystal's three parental figures involved, somebody wasn't telling everything they knew. And wasn't that the case in every one of these unsolved crimes she'd come across? Somebody involved had kept their secret, sometimes to the grave. This wasn't a case of a child getting washed down a river; this was a case of somebody deliberately stealing the child from her bedroom during the night.

As Doreen thought about all that, she considered a wild possibility.

What if Crystal herself had wanted to disappear?

What if she was uncomfortable with her father and her stepmother? What if somebody gave her an out? She was only eight. Would she have taken off from her mother? And, if her father had a girlfriend, did her mother have a boyfriend? Was there a pedophile who had slipped in under the radar who decided Crystal was his perfect next victim? There were just so many questions and so few answers that Doreen knew once again it would be hard to find the truth without poking some of those very nasty, long-held secrets.

The first thing was to look up the people involved, and, in a way, Mack was likely to be the best one to find answers on Guido. And Eric, for that matter. She frowned as she made herself a cup of tea. Just as she was about to sit back down, she felt compelled to call Mack to apologize. She hated to admit when she was wrong, but ... she grabbed her phone and dialed him.

"Why'd you call? So you can hang up on me again?" he asked, his tone dry. "Or do you want something again?"

At that, she winced and stopped. She didn't even know how to proceed.

"You do want something, don't you?" he said, his tone suddenly weary.

"Not for the reason you think though," she said gently. "Of course I have information I need from you. But, if I can help you solve this case, which obviously weighs heavy on your heart, I would like to do so. And I wanted to apologize."

She was startled by the silence at the other end of the phone. "Thank you. I didn't say it weighed on my heart," he said, his tone suddenly brisk.

"You don't have to be the big tough guy all the time. Obviously you were affected by Crystal's disappearance, but there should be answers we can find. I don't have any skills at this. Just beginner's luck. But, if you let me turn a light on this case, maybe—just maybe—I can help."

"Maybe," he said, but his tone was reluctant. "But you have to share everything with me. These men are dangerous. You can't get into another situation like you keep getting into."

"I'm not trying to get into them," she said carefully. "But Guido has a record, and I believe Eric does too because he was involved in the theft of stolen goods."

"Guido, Guido, Guido …" Mack's tone trailed off as he thought about that. "I don't know that name."

"Mary's brother, along with José. So Nan was talking to him, and he wasn't clear but mentioned blackmail."

"What?" Mack said. "Whoa, whoa, let's go back to the beginning. What is this about blackmail?"

Doreen told him the details, this time about what Nan had said.

"So you think Mary wanted to get rid of Crystal and used her brothers to do so, but they wanted something for their time, so they came up with the blackmail scheme?"

"That's possible, yes. What I don't know, and hear me out on this," she said before he could rush in to ask more questions, "is whether that child was aware enough of the adults in her life to understand this might happen and if she left them or if she was a victim."

Mack's shocked silence hung in the air. "Okay, so now you've got a bunch of running theories."

"You know me," Doreen said humorously. "I pull out every bizarre counterintuitive theory and give it a good shake to see what rattles out."

"The trouble is, when you give things a good shake," he said, "yes, some things rattle out, but sometimes you get hurt in the process, and so do other people."

"And I said I'll be careful," she said. "But I can't sit in a bubble, if there's anything I can do to help Crystal."

"You really think she's alive?"

"Not necessarily. I don't have any proof of that. But I have to wonder."

"Bizarre," he said.

"What I need from you are addresses ..."

"No way," Mack said. "If these guys have criminal records, and if they are involved in this kidnapping case, there's absolutely no way you should drive by and push their buttons. When those buttons get pushed, they'll explode, and they will do anything to stop you from finding out the truth."

"Oh, I get that. So I want you to do the drive-by," she said triumphantly.

"What?" he asked in a dry tone. "You can't just jump in here and try to be a superwoman again."

"I'd love to do a drive-by with you," she said cheerfully. "But, as long as you do the drive-by, and maybe put some pressure on them, ... if they see you, they'll wonder what's going on. That'll rattle some bones too."

"Not really. These people aren't full of sweetness and light. They're probably used to seeing the cops around."

"Maybe, but now you've got a second case with a second footprint and potentially a second child involved."

"I know," he said, "but I still haven't figured out the connection between the two cases."

"You have the connection," she said. "You just don't understand the motive. Why go in and take the child's stuff and not the child? Why take the child and a few things ten years ago and leave the same footprint?"

Silence.

"Did you ever track down what kind of a footprint it was?" she asked.

"No," he said, "we haven't. Why?"

"Because that'll be the key to this, obviously," she said in exasperation, noting his voice was deliberately bland. She groaned. "But, of course, you know this, and you're saying anything you can to keep me off the trail."

"I'm trying to keep you safe," he said. "Something you're determined to not let me do."

"That's not quite true," she said. "I'm happy to stay safe, but you have to consider two children's rooms, one child gone, one child left alone, the same perpetrator, just means there'll be a third one."

"What, in ten years again?"

"I'm not sure ten years is significant," she said. "And can you search to see if there's anything similar in Vernon or in Penticton or even Vancouver?"

"We're on it," Mack said, his tone brisk again. "I'll check into this Guido's and Eric's prison records. I don't know what exactly is on their rap sheet at this point. I have to refresh my memory. And I'll leave now," he said cheerfully. "You have an empty house and need some food."

"I was wondering if you were up for another cooking lesson sometime soon," she said hesitantly. "I could pay for the groceries this time."

At that, he chuckled. "Feeling guilty or just really hungry?"

"Both, even though I ate not long ago," she said with spirit. "And I don't want to push you because I know how busy you are. I have to do some shopping though, so, if I knew what to pick up, I could buy it."

"There's not a lot I can't cook," Mack said, "or I can't figure out how to cook, so why don't you see what you would like to have. Today is only Tuesday, so, if you buy some fresh meat, it won't keep all that long. We'd have to cook it Wednesday, Thursday, or Friday, although planning for a Friday night dinner wouldn't be a bad idea."

"Fresh, like what?"

"Like, chicken for example. Or ribs don't keep terribly long, so they would need to be eaten before the weekend."

"Okay, well, I have to go out maybe tomorrow. I'm too tired to do anything tonight, especially after the visit with Nan. Maybe I'll shop in the morning. I have to take more stuff to Wendy's too."

At that, he laughed again.

She frowned. "What are you laughing at now?"

"Is there anything left in the house?"

She sighed. "There's still too damn much. But I haven't made it into the garage or to the basement yet, so I have no idea what to do with some of the stuff that's still left behind."

"If what you have left is not valuable," he said, "then maybe one of the donation places would come and pick it all up. You'd have to have it all at the end of the driveway, or maybe, in special circumstances, you could just have it in the garage, open the door for them, and they could load it. I think it has to be boxed though."

"Even that would be a huge help," she said, "just to empty the house, to have it *completely* empty, then I could figure out what to put back in."

"You'll have nothing to put back in," he said. "You'll have to start shopping."

"Would garage sales be a place to do that kind of shopping?" she asked curiously. "I kind of need a printer stand now because that hutch is gone. I need a desk or something to fit in that alcove. That is something I have to look at. I have no dressers. I don't have a bed ..."

"There was a spare bed upstairs. What about that one?"

"I wish they'd taken that," she said. "The springs are

gone, and it's rickety, and it makes a ton of noise."

"If you want to get rid of it, we can take it to the dump."

"That wouldn't be a bad idea. You know what I'm thinking?" she asked. "Maybe I should just go room by room, bring everything I don't want and I'm not keeping into the garage. Empty the entire house, move it all into the garage, see what I can give away, and, if you would help," she added, "I could pay you for a dump run. But it would be nice to finally get this done."

"You've been at it for weeks, haven't you?" he asked. "And you've accomplished a ton."

"I know, but there's still a lot left."

"We'll start upstairs in the bathrooms and the bedrooms, bring it all down, and then maybe sort out what's left in the basement. Let's get all that upstairs done first."

"Speaking of that storage area below the living room, any chance Crystal's house had a secret space?"

"I don't think so," he said. "Why would there be?"

"What if she disappeared on her own or with her mother's help or, or, or ..." she said, throwing up her hand. "I don't know. I'm just wondering. I never knew hatches like that existed until Nan's house. So now my mind can't stop thinking of the possibilities."

"Sure, that's possible," Mack said, "but outside of hiding an intruder, I doubt that's where the child's body would be hidden. The decomp would have been horrific."

"What if she was in on her kidnapping, her disappearance?" Doreen asked, her mind reaching for answers. "What if she was getting something out of this?"

"Away from her parents is the only thing she'd get out of it."

"Exactly," Doreen said on a thoughtful note. "We only

have the parents' word that they had a great relationship with her. What if it was the opposite? What if the stepmother and/or father abused her?"

"And the mother?"

That stopped her. "True," she said. "I can't imagine Clara abusing Crystal. But we don't know what people are like behind closed doors. Also did Clara have a boyfriend at the time? That was one of the other questions I meant to ask you in case her boyfriend was preying on Crystal."

"I don't like the way your mind thinks," he said.

"You might not," she said, "but I'm pretty sure you guys already thought of that angle."

"Yes, because that's one of the first things we consider when a child goes missing. We couldn't find anything at the time, that much I do know."

"Maybe you could go through the file and send me anything you're allowed to send me, and, no, I don't want you to get into trouble. I'll do some research at the library, see what I can come up with," she said cheerfully. "But not today."

Just as she went to hang up, he said, "And tomorrow you'll buy groceries for a Friday night dinner, right?"

"Correct," she said. "I'll let you know what I pick up."

And she hung up.

Chapter 23

Wednesday Morning ...

THE NEXT MORNING Doreen woke up full of determination and energy. She finished off the closet in her bedroom, taking everything she wasn't keeping to the garage, stopping to admire the fact that the garage was now ninety-nine percent empty, and started stacking up donation stuff on the floor.

She went back upstairs, her bedroom now mostly empty. She had the bed—still just a mattress and a box spring on the floor—and the clothes she had decided to keep were hung up in her nice, mostly empty closet. Then she went to the spare bedroom, sorted through all the clothes she'd put in there. Those she wouldn't keep joined the others in the boxes or bags in the garage. The rest, those she would keep, were promptly hung up in the master bedroom closet.

She walked once more into the spare bedroom, eyeing what was left. The spare room did have a night table, and she figured she could use that, so she moved it and the lamp to her bedroom and set it up beside the mattress on the floor. The spare bed was pretty nasty, but, for the moment, it would have to stay here as it was too big for her to handle alone. There was also a dresser, and it was in decent shape. She took out the drawers and then manhandled the piece into her bedroom. She put it against the wall between the two windows; then she grabbed the drawers and put them back in. Now she'd made herself something of a bedroom. She had left the spare room pretty empty, but she didn't expect to have any company, so she had no real need for a functional guest bedroom.

Happier, she checked the master en suite bathroom and saw some things of Nan's still here. She grabbed a couple more boxes and an old laundry hamper and emptied everything from the cupboards, so just Doreen's stuff was stored here. Then she went to the other bathroom and did the same thing. She took everything that wasn't hers downstairs to the kitchen, thinking she'd just toss these old bath and beauty items.

She put on coffee and fed the animals, then took her coffee outside to take a new look at the garden. A ladder still rested against the backside of the garage, laying on the long side on the grass. Not the wisest thing for a single woman living alone to leave outside, to give intruders this handy access to her second floor. She had no heavy-duty hooks inside the garage to hang this ladder up on a wall. Something else to add to her to-do list. She looked at the feet to the ladder, how each wobbled back and forth, so it could adjust to uneven ground.

She thought about that some more, thinking how one would carry an eight-year-old out of a bedroom, either asleep or unconscious. Even if the window was four feet high, it would still be awkward to get the dead weight of a drugged or sleeping child outside, or easier to carry a willing child than to let her climb the ladder herself. No matter what, it seemed a ladder would have been necessary. And, therefore, a ladder would have left its own footprint.

She picked up the phone, and, before Mack had a chance to say anything, she said, "You realize that odd footprint is the broken foot of a ladder, right?"

"We considered that," he said, "and good morning to you. That's not a normal footprint for a ladder."

"Maybe not a normal one," she said, still eyeing her ladder, "but it'll be very identifiable. You just have to find it."

"Thank you very much for the lesson in police work," he said in exasperation. "Did you eat yet?"

She frowned at her phone. "What does me eating have to do with ladders?"

"It has to do with your snappiness," he said with a note of humor. "It sounds like you're hungry."

She brushed her hair off her face. "I haven't eaten," she said. "I've been working hard. I cleaned up everything from the upstairs and brought the donations to the garage, moved the night table and dresser from the spare bedroom into my bedroom so I have more storage space for my own stuff. I haven't fully unpacked my suitcases, which is something I still need to do, but I called it quits for now."

"You also need a bed frame for your room or to get rid of that old bed potentially," he said. "Probably should get rid of both old beds up there."

"That'll depend on money. It's kind of nice to have a spare bed in case of company, but I don't know who the heck I would have stay here."

"But you never know," he said cheerfully. "Go get food." This time he hung up on her.

At that, she laughed. "Did that feel good?" she asked Mack out loud. "Because it kind of sucks on my end." She pocketed her phone, walked back inside, and made herself some toast with peanut butter. Then she walked through to the garage again, took a careful look at the remaining furniture, and noted a few chairs and a table that looked to be broken. She put it all at the end of the garage, off to the side.

With that done, she opened the double doors and headed downstairs to the basement. At the base of the stairs, she stopped and gasped. The big room was empty except for a couple pieces around the corner. She'd have to go through the paperwork and make sure, but this was incredible. It was also very freeing. It was like the house had been given a new life, a huge weight off its shoulders. And hers.

She went around the corner into the cold room, and still a bunch of the kitchen stuff was here, but a lot of it had gone with the movers too. Maybe Agatha took it; Doreen didn't know. Again she hadn't gone through the Christie's paperwork yet. She certainly wasn't much of a business person, was she? Frowning at that, she turned on more of the lights and took a few photos to make sure she knew what was here now. She shut off the lights and walked back to the kitchen. The stack of paperwork, documenting the transfer from her house to Christie's, was large in front of her, and most pages listed multiple items. It would take her a few hours to sort that out. She needed an office to keep her more organized— or at least a desk.

She had seen a broken desk in the basement. She wondered if that was fixable. She headed back downstairs. Although the desk was relatively nice, the face on one of the drawers had come off along with one leg—but she found both pieces nearby. She studied the desk for a long moment and called Mack back. "You any good with tools?"

"I guess it depends what kind," he said with a humorous note. "What's broken?"

"The movers didn't leave much downstairs in the basement, but there's a desk, missing a faceplate to a drawer and one leg. I think it might fit in that alcove space where I need something for the printer."

"Measure it," he instructed. "And when I come over on Friday, I'll see if we can put it together and get it in place."

"I do have tools," she cried out cheerfully. "I just don't know how to use them."

"You might find YouTube helpful," he said, chuckling, and again he hung up on her.

She went to the garage and looked around for a tape measure. She found one in a drawer, although the drawer itself seemed a little wobbly and wouldn't slide back inside properly like it was supposed to. She headed into the kitchen and back to the little alcove area there. She measured the space on both sides and then headed into the basement to measure the desk. She cried out in triumph when she realized it would fit. "Now that would be perfect."

She looked at the drawer and at the missing faceplate; it just needed screws and it'd fit right back on. She looked at the backside of the faceplate to the other drawers and thought she understood how it went together. Taking the drawer to the workshop, she put it on one of the benches and searched in the drawers for screws. Finding one, she didn't know what the hell she was supposed to do now. Hating to ask Mack, she headed back inside and looked it up on YouTube. And, sure enough, it was all about screwdrivers.

She identified the correct head and what she was supposed to do with it, and she just laughed. "All you do is turn it," she said. She hunted through her tools and found a screwdriver that fit her screw and carefully placed the pieces together and twisted in the screw. And it worked. It was a slightly bigger screw than the hole; maybe that was why it worked. Maybe the drawer face had come off because the hole had been stripped, or whatever the case might have been. In her mind, she could see the logic of it, and the drawer seemed to be holding together just fine.

She left the drawer there and then brought up the other drawers to the kitchen, and, on her last trip, she carried the broken desk out to the garage. Studying the way the other legs were attached to the desk, she fixed the broken leg too. She was beside herself with joy. She'd repaired it! By herself. Without Mack. She'd also taken pictures every step of the way. She sent the pictures to Mack and then a selfie with her beaming, standing beside the desk in the garage.

When he called her a few moments later, he said, "Wow. Very enterprising and a great job."

The surprise in his voice made her wince. "You didn't think I could do it, did you?"

"I knew you could," he said. "I just didn't know if you would make the effort to try."

"I might have done myself in though," she said. "I'm not certain I can fit the desk in that corner."

"You did measure it first?"

"I did," she said. She had the phone tucked against her ear, and she lifted the empty desk again. "It's pretty heavy even without the drawers though," she complained good-naturedly. "Good thing it's not a massive desk."

"Don't hurt yourself," he warned.

"Mack," she said, "if I lived the way you want me to, I wouldn't have any fun at all."

"Ha," he said. "There's a big difference between getting in a murderer's face and accusing him of crimes that will send him away for the next twenty years versus lifting a desk." Just then the desk slipped out of her hands and came crashing down. His voice came through the phone. "Hey, are you okay? What was that?"

"I'm fine," she said. "And the desk held. Now I just have to drag it and drop it into the right place. I'll talk to you later," she said, and she hung up the phone.

The reason she'd stumbled was because of Goliath, trying to help. She looked down at him and groaned. "Goliath, you're not supposed to be under the desk. Let me get it into place. Then you can hop on the desk."

It took a bit of maneuvering, but she did get it inside the kitchen and down to the end of the alcove. Instead of putting it at the end so she faced the wall, she put it under the window so she could see outside. She was huffing and puffing by the time she was done, but she hooked the printer back up, set her laptop on the desk, along with the stack of papers from the kitchen dining area.

That left her table clear, since John had taken a large stack of the old books, but she didn't remember him saying he would take them all. She had taken photos of the spines, so she knew which ones had been here, and she could only hope these men were trustworthy. She'd learned a lot in the last year since separating from her husband and now knew people weren't always as honest as she wanted them to be.

Chapter 24

Wednesday Late Morning…

AS DOREEN WORKED around the house, her thoughts returned to Crystal. Doreen really didn't know a lot about the little girl. The internet didn't offer anything except bits and pieces of news flashes about her kidnapping case, about all the searchers out looking for her, the hunt going on, and how the police vowed they'd not rest until they found her. No mention of Mack was found anywhere in there, but then he was probably like everyone else, ten years younger back then. She pulled out her phone and sent Clara a message, asking if Crystal's room was still the same as when she'd left.

Instead of texting, Clara phoned her. When Doreen answered, Clara said, "I haven't touched her room, and, as far as I know, my husband hasn't touched her bedroom in his house either. Why? Why does it matter?"

"It doesn't," Doreen said. "I would just like to know a lot more about Crystal, and that's one way to do so."

"When I'm off work, which is in about an hour," Clara said abruptly, "I can meet you at my house. And I'll show you."

"Okay," Doreen said. "I'll come up with the animals. I'll leave here in a bit and meet you at home." With that, she hung up, glanced around her house and considered that maybe, instead of walking with the animals, she should drive there and go shopping afterward, like she had already told Mack she would do, and then come home to put away the perishable foods.

Not certain about when to go to the store yet, she realized she also hadn't gone to the bank. That put a little spark into her feet as she hopped up, grabbed her purse, and locked the animals inside. In her car, she pulled into the cul-de-sac and drove to the bank. She hadn't been to a bank very often—she usually dealt with investors, and they had very different offices.

When she walked in, one of the tellers looked up and smiled. "May I help you?"

Relieved, Doreen pulled out the large stack of cash from her purse and handed it over. And then, finding her bank card, she handed it over too. She watched the process anxiously, but it didn't seem to take anything at all to accomplish this.

The woman asked, "Do you need any cash?"

"No," Doreen said. "I have lots with me." She opened her wallet wider to show her the stash of cash she still had.

The bank teller looked at the money and frowned. "Do you want to put some of that in the bank?"

Doreen hesitated.

"If you want to keep it, that's fine too," the teller said. "But don't leave that kind of money in your wallet, just in case you lose it. And don't let other people see that cash in your wallet either."

On that note, realizing she had a grand in her wallet,

FOOTPRINTS IN THE FERNS

Doreen pulled out the five hundred from the sale of the two chairs and asked, "Can you deposit this too, please?"

The teller did so and gave her a receipt, showing how much money she now had in her account. Then Doreen, remembering her unpaid bills, pulled them from her purse, and asked if the teller would transfer the funds to pay these.

She smiled sweetly and said, "I'll set these up online and take care of that right now. It'll only take a minute or two. Then you should be able to make next month's payment from your home computer."

Doreen wasn't sure how to do that yet, and she didn't want to ask Mack about it and get laughed at again, but she felt certain she could find instructions somewhere on YouTube.

"Okay, you're all set. At least for these two bills. As you get other bills, just add them into your bank account information online, as people or utilities or loans or whatever to be paid."

"Thank you so much." Doreen turned and exited the bank. Relieved and feeling quite proud of herself, Doreen looked at the receipt, smiling at the thirty-five hundred in her bank account. "Nan, that's a heck of a lot of money all of a sudden. Especially for somebody who's starving."

Speaking of which, she was off to the grocery store next. As she walked into the store, pushing her cart ahead of her, she glanced around. Many times when she'd been here, she had seen people she knew, and sometimes they were helpful to her cold cases work. She really didn't know who she was supposed to talk to in this case though, but still that weird suspicion remained in the back of her mind. She had no reason for this to be her primary theory, but she was desperate for it to be right.

What if Crystal was alive? Why would she have not tried to contact her mother? Or her father? The first thoughts that came up were either she didn't want to or she couldn't. And then Doreen thought about all the different things the little girl may have gone through in the years since she had been removed from her bedroom and how hard it would be to call the people who were supposed to look after her but didn't.

Was there anything inside that little girl that wanted to call her family? Doreen just couldn't seem to figure this mess out.

She picked up the basics for sandwiches, cheese and crackers, more cat food—Goliath the monster was going through more food than the rest of them. She got some doggy treats, knowing Mugs would absolutely love a little bit more money flowing into their household. She found a few canned goods, like tuna, and added coffee to her cart. Thankfully that was on sale, and she bought three packages, feeling incredibly abundant as she did so, knowing she was perfectly capable of paying for this. Coffee was something she never wanted to end up short on.

As she stood in front of the meat section, she worried about what to get. She didn't know how long things took to cook, so she didn't know if some things weren't possible for Friday night dinner when it came to a big piece of meat, like a roast or a whole chicken. There were ribs, but she kind of thought they had to be dealt with differently. She didn't have a barbecue—wouldn't that have been nice? But that wasn't in her budget. She wandered along until she came to some pork chops and thought she would enjoy them again, plus they should be fairly easy to cook.

She grabbed a pack and found some preformed and mar-inated burgers, if you read the packaging. They were also on sale. They looked to be a hell of a deal, so she put those in her buggy too. Surely Mack could show her how to cook them. She wandered along, grabbing eggs and more veggies. Mentally calculating how much she'd spent, she was still under the hundred dollars she had budgeted for groceries. After bagging the groceries and putting them back in the basket, she was feeling positively spry.

As she walked outside, Steve walked in. He frowned at her and slipped past.

She glared at him. "Was that you in my backyard the other night?" she cried out. Several people stopped to look as she raised her voice.

Steve glanced around. "You know nothing. You're just a lonely old busybody," he snapped. "You don't know anything." And he disappeared.

She frowned, not really liking the man at all but didn't have any reason to call the cops on him. Just because he'd been in her backyard wasn't a criminal offense. It was probably trespassing, but she could hardly get Mack to do something about that when much more important issues were ahead of them. There was just something about Steve … Something she didn't like. Something that was off … She turned back to see him standing there, glaring at her.

With a bright smile she waved at him. No way she would show him that she was unnerved by his presence. Much better that he be nervous of her and what she was up to …

Chapter 25

Wednesday Noon ...

DOREEN CAUGHT SIGHT of a whisper across Steve's face, a whisper of fear or a whisper of maybe panic? And then he schooled his features to just glare at her. "You don't know anything." And this time he took off down the aisle.

One of the women watching the play by play with interest said, "Is he involved in one of your cold cases, dear?"

Doreen looked at the woman who had more purple in her hair than the royal purple shirt she wore and smiled. "I'm not sure," she said, "but maybe."

The old woman nodded. "I wouldn't doubt it. He's a dodgy one."

"In what way?" Doreen asked.

"Three wives," the woman announced. "First one disappeared, second one took off, and then the third one, well, nobody has seen her for years."

Doreen froze. "What?"

The woman went off in peals of laughter. "He didn't kill them though," she said with a big chuckle. "I was just having some fun with you. His first wife took off with another man.

The second one he ditched in town, and they split up soon after. No clue what happened to the third one, but I'm sure she made a better decision than to hang around him." And, at that, she took off, pushing her buggy, half bent over the small cart with a big smirk on her face.

Doreen stared at her in fascination. "What the heck did that mean?" she asked. Of course she would love to find something creepy or criminal in Steve's past to confirm how something was off about him. The fact that he was hanging around her now and was friends with Penny, already in jail for murder, was disturbing enough. Doreen had caught somebody in her backyard, but she didn't know who it was, and, of course, she and Steve had already had their altercations. That didn't mean he had anything to do with this current case. But she filed it away—you never knew what might come down the road.

Worrying about the craziness of some of the local, more colorful people, she wandered back to her vehicle, packed up, and made a quick dash home to unload what food needed to be refrigerated. Mugs could smell his treats, even in their unopened packaging. "I'll give you something special when I return. Okay, Mugs?" Then, checking her watch, she would be late if she didn't get a move on to Clara's place. Driving carefully, she finally pulled in front of Clara's house, parked, and got out. Clara was waiting on the front step for her. Doreen rushed ahead, apologizing. "I'm so sorry. The grocery shopping took a little longer than I expected."

"I thought you were going to walk," Clara said curiously, looking around. "You don't have any of the animals?"

"No. I was out of time, so I came straight here from home, after putting up the meat in the fridge," Doreen said.

Clara shrugged and let her into the house. "Come

through here to the bedroom."

As Doreen followed Clara down the hallway, she saw a master on the left and a small bedroom on the far back right. "Did you have a boyfriend at the time Crystal disappeared?"

Clara gave her a sharp look. "Yes, I did," she said. "I was finding my feminine side again. Nothing like being replaced to make you feel like you don't have what it takes anymore."

Doreen didn't say anything because that certainly hadn't been her instinctive reaction as a way to handle it, but she knew a lot of women who immediately went out and found new relationships. She'd heard the term "hump and dump them," but that was too rude and crude for her.

She stepped into the little girl's bedroom, and it was like going back in time. "Have you taken anything out of here since then?"

"No, it's exactly the same as when she disappeared," Clara admitted. "I left it so that, when she came back, it would feel like home. But, of course, the real truth of the matter is, I have no idea if she's ever coming back. And, when she does, it's already been ten years, so she's eighteen. There isn't anything she wants here now."

"I don't know about that," Doreen said. "I can't even begin to speak to her mind-set. But I do think, knowing you've kept all her stuff still, that will probably make her feel very nice."

"I doubt it," Clara said with a note of bitterness. "I'd love to believe she's alive. But, if she is, why wouldn't she have contacted me?"

"Only two reasons come to mind," Doreen said carefully. She stepped forward to the bed, sitting down at the edge, her hands going to the pillow. "Either she couldn't or she didn't want to." On that last bit, she stole a glance sideways at Clara to see her face twist. "Is there any reason why she wouldn't want to?"

Clara looked at her and frowned. "I don't think I like what you're suggesting."

"I'm not suggesting anything," Doreen said quietly. "And you know perfectly well the police have asked much worse."

"Isn't that the truth," Clara cried out. "They suggested all kinds of horrible things back in the day."

"I'm sure they did," Doreen said, "but, in reality, they did so for Crystal's benefit. When they're trying to find a child, they want to make sure they turn over every stone."

"Well, they scared my boyfriend away at the time too," Clara snapped.

"What was his name?" Doreen asked. She had her phone out, and she put it on Audio and Video.

"Tom Delaware. I really, really liked him," she said with a heavy sigh. "But I don't know that it would have lasted."

"Why didn't he stick around?"

"He didn't like the police digging into our lives," she said. "He was on the run from an ex-wife and kids and didn't want to pay child support. I didn't know that at the time, of course, so it was a bit disconcerting when he took off with that as his excuse."

"He told you that was his excuse before he left?" Doreen asked curiously. "That's kind of odd, isn't it? Wouldn't he have tried to avoid telling you why he was leaving?"

"I have no idea," she said.

"How long had you known him before he took off?"

"Just a few months but we were only close for a few weeks. It was really tough for a while there. And, with my daughter going back and forth between my place and her father's, for the first time, I had some freedom. Some evenings to myself where I could pursue a relationship. So I did. And it went on until my daughter disappeared, and everything blew up. It would have been nice if Tom had stuck around to help me get through it, but he didn't, and so I had that to deal with as well."

"What was your relationship like with your husband during that time?"

"Caring mostly, although there were some arguments, but nothing serious," she admitted. "For a while there I wondered if all our problems were under the bridge and if we would get back together again, but it didn't happen. Mary was firmly entrenched in his life and in his home, and she made sure we didn't get any closer to each other."

"Was he equally devastated at Crystal's disappearance?"

"Yes," Clara said abruptly. "I know the police looked into him very carefully, but they never found anything. And I truly believe he was devastated and wouldn't have done anything to hurt her. She was our only child, and he's never had any children with anyone else, so now we're both childless." A sob escaped from her throat.

"You've never wanted to have any more?" Doreen asked.

"I've wanted to," she said. "But how do you move on from something like that? I also didn't have a relationship, so that didn't help. I didn't want to be a single parent. I wanted to be a parent to Crystal with Eric. It was really tough."

"Have you got any working theories as to what happened?"

"I had lots back then, but now, over time, it makes me wonder if I saw anything clearly," she said, sitting down beside Doreen on the bed, her hand grabbing a handful of the comforter and squeezing it tight. "I still think Mary had something to do with it though."

"What about friends? Did Crystal have any close friends?"

"She did at first but not really after we separated. None of her friends' parents were going through divorces, and it was very difficult for those parents to understand what we were going through, and the other parents didn't want their own children to witness Crystal's parents splitting up. I don't know what to say, but, for a long time, Crystal didn't want to come home anymore."

"Ouch," Doreen said. "That would have made it very difficult."

"It did," Clara said. "I mean, how do you handle that?"

"Did she want to go to her father's then?"

"She told me that she didn't want to be with either of us until we stopped fighting. And we did fight, but it was just our relationship. And she didn't like having two homes. She always wanted to see what the other was having for dinner before she would settle into eating dinner at one place or the other. But she didn't like Mary, I know that."

"Any idea why?"

Clara just shrugged and said, "No, not really. Crystal said she didn't like the way Mary looked at her sometimes."

Doreen nodded. "I think children, like animals, have a strong instinct when it comes to people. She may very well not have gotten along with Mary, but that doesn't mean Mary had anything to do with her disappearance."

"No, but it also doesn't mean she didn't."

"Do you want Mary to be guilty?" Doreen asked point-blank. "Because that's what it sounds like."

Clara sobbed for a moment and then choked it back. She stood, wrapped her arms around her chest, and paced the small room. "It's all I could think about at the time. And I don't know if that was misplaced anger on my part because ultimately Mary split us up," she said. "My husband told me that he wanted a younger woman, and he wanted to be with Mary, not with me."

"Ah, so it wasn't a mutual breakup?"

"Well, I definitely wanted to break up when I found out he was already sleeping with her. But before that? No. I was doing everything I could to save my marriage. But he had already hooked up with Mary, and he's never looked back."

"How long were you married?"

"Ten years," she said on a bitter laugh. "As long as he's been with Mary now. For me, those years just seem like a long time ago because I haven't really moved on. I haven't filled the ten years since with anything good, whereas he's had a brand-new relationship to help him get through it."

"So you were married to him when he was criminally charged?"

At that, Clara sat down with a heavy sag. "Yes," she said, "technically, yes. I didn't realize what he was doing. He says he didn't understand or think that he'd get caught. He ran a pawn shop where people would bring him stuff, and he'd try to resell it online. He did a lot on eBay and websites like that."

"I'm sorry," Doreen said, but she didn't understand. "So you didn't have any part in it?"

Clara's back stiffened. "No," she said. "I never really thought about where he got this stuff. He said he picked it up in auction lots and things like that. But obviously he was lying, but then he lied about a lot of things, like Mary, for instance."

Doreen waited to see if more explanations were coming.

And then finally Clara raised both hands in frustration and said, "It doesn't really make much difference, but apparently he was with Mary for several months before we split, and then he broke it off with her while we were splitting up. Then, all of a sudden, Mary moved into the house. That was my house, you know?" she said with a sad look at Doreen. "I bought this one afterward with my mother's help. So I could stay close. I told myself it was so I could stay close to my daughter, and that was true, but I also wanted to stay close to my husband, but that just made it worse when he and Mary got together publicly. She moved into the house as soon as she could. I swear, she moved in the night I moved out. I was pretty upset for a long time."

"I'm sure it affected Crystal."

"Maybe," she said, "but *I* didn't have anything to do with her disappearance."

"Is there anybody who would have helped her run away and stay away all this time?"

Clara just stared at her. "What do you mean?"

"I mean, is there anybody—family, friends, grandparents—who would have given her a home and not told you what they were doing?"

"No, absolutely not. We're all very close."

Doreen just smiled and nodded but didn't say anything because *very close* didn't sound like what Clara was describing. "Is there any reason Crystal would want to get away from the family?"

"I know she wanted to get away from Mary."

"And yet, she didn't sleep here all the time, did she?"

Clara's shoulders slumped at that truth, but she shook her head and said, "No, you're right. She'd always go back again to Eric's house, where Mary was."

"So, how bad was it really over there?"

"Probably not as bad as I wanted it to be," Clara said. "Maybe I just built it up more in my mind because I don't like the woman."

Doreen privately thought that was likely true. "What about at school? Was anybody bothering her, like a school bully? Did she have a problem with a teacher or the principal or any adult?"

Clara just stared at her. "I don't like that question either," she said. "As far as I know, nobody would have kidnapped her and hurt her or helped her escape from me and my husband."

"Good," Doreen said briskly. "That's what I needed to know." She wasn't going to mention any suggestion of abuse. She figured the police could handle that part of this mess.

Clara straightened up and said, "Look. I'll put on a pot of coffee. I presume you want a few minutes to just check out her room."

"Absolutely," Doreen said with a smile. She waited until Clara was gone and then went through the dresser and the night table. A diary would have been lovely, but Crystal had been only eight so maybe young for such an activity. And if she had chance, her mother would have gone through anything like that pretty carefully. Doreen checked under the sheets and between the mattresses and behind the dresser and pulled out the drawers and checked behind there too. Going through Nan's stuff had taught her all that. Finally, by the time Clara returned, Doreen stood in the room with her hands on her hips.

"Did you find anything?"

"No," Doreen said. "Obviously, if something were hidden here, the cops would have found it long ago."

"Exactly," Clara said.

"There're no pictures on the wall," Doreen noted. "No stuffed animals on the bed. No dolls on the floor. Did you pack up any of her things?"

Clara shook her head.

"It's almost like she didn't have a personality."

"She slept here, that's for sure," her mom said. "She did a lot of homework here on her computer."

"Where's her computer?"

Clara shook her head. "I don't know. I thought about that, but I don't have a clue where it is. I asked Eric about it, and he said he thought it was with me."

"A laptop?" Doreen asked.

Clara nodded. "Her father bought it for her."

"That's a pretty expensive gift for a young girl."

"Oh, it wasn't new," Clara said. "It was one more of those things he used to buy and sell."

"Ah," Doreen said. "Any idea if she took it to the mall or with her to her friends' houses?"

"She took it with her everywhere. Sometimes she and her friends would sit in these little parks and play games together on each other's laptops. They also took them to the library downtown."

"Right," Doreen said. "Any idea when Crystal's laptop might have gone missing?"

"No, but I figured it must have been that same night. Because it's not at my place, and it's not at his. So where else could it be?"

"That means it was important to her if she took it with her."

"Or somebody understood she played with it or thought

there might be incriminating evidence on it," Clara said, "and took it with them."

"Right," Doreen said as she cast a final glance around the room. "I guess there's no chance to get into her room in her father's house, is there?"

Clara looked at her in surprise. "Actually there is. They're gone for the week, and I'm looking after the plants and the cat."

"Oh, you're that good a friend?"

"I am with my husband. I tolerate Mary."

Clara was still using the term *husband*, not *ex-husband*, which Doreen thought very odd. And very sad. Clara's view on their married relationship sounded at odds with the arguing she had mentioned as well. Maybe she still loved her ex-husband? Still wanted him back enough to gloss over the fighting? "Would you mind? I'd like to take a quick look."

"I guess that's even more important because that's where she was taken from."

"Yes," Doreen said. They exited Clara's house and walked across the street. Eric's house was almost a matching bungalow on the other side.

Clara let them in the front door and said, "I have to clean the litter box and feed the cat anyway. Go down that hallway. Crystal's room is at the end."

Doreen wasted no time. She headed toward Crystal's room, curious to see just what this was all about. As she stepped inside, she saw another room stuck in time. She stood with her hands on her hips, wondering how she would handle such a thing. *Would I keep it as a shrine to my lost child? Would I keep it with everything exactly as she left it, hoping she'd come back and remember this was home? Would I lock the door to her room, so I didn't have to see it every day? Would I pack it all up, store it in the attic, and convert this room to a guest room or as an exercise room?* All of it seemed psychologically damaging no matter which way you went.

Doreen went through the closets and through the bed and the dressers. She saw a few toys, but not much was here either. She'd have to ask for that list of toys that disappeared with her. And was the laptop even on that list? How many eight-year-olds had their own laptop? She frowned at that, thinking it was fairly odd. Especially ten years ago, when they were quite pricey. Then again her father likely got a "deal," and, chances were, it wasn't in great condition.

As Doreen went through the closet, she found it went quite deep. She pushed all the clothes and the hangers off to one side and stepped farther in, using the flashlight on her phone.

In the back on a set of shelves was a small box. She pulled the box into the room and took a look at it. It was an old laptop box and still had some manuals and things in it. She flipped through it all, but there wasn't much except the serial number. She took a photo of that, replaced the box, and pulled another box from the shelf.

She found some old cards from classmates and family members, but she found nothing important until she got to the bottom of the stack—a picture of Crystal and several other people. They all appeared to be happy. She was held aloft by two big men, and a woman stood beside them. She pulled out the photo as Clara walked into the room. Doreen held it up and asked, "When was this taken?"

Clara stared at it. "I never saw that before."

"Is that Mary?"

Clara nodded and asked, "Who are the men beside her?"

The two women looked at the photo, and Clara burst out, "Oh, that's José and Guido, Mary's brothers."

Chapter 26

Wednesday Early Afternoon ...

BACK IN HER vehicle, Doreen went around the block, parked, then got out, and went to the corner of the road to see what Clara might do next. Doreen watched as Clara walked across to her house and then appeared to be inside for a while. Wondering if she was wrong, Doreen sat and waited. And then, all of a sudden, Clara's vehicle came ripping down the block. She didn't even look in Doreen's direction and tore around the corner.

Doreen hopped back into her car, following Clara as best she could from a distance. Clara appeared to be on a mission, but Doreen had no idea what mission or why. She took lefts and then rights, headed through the main part of town, until they climbed a hill heading toward the Clifton Road area. Doreen frowned, realizing they were heading toward Glenmore—wasn't that where one of the brothers lived? At least that's what Nan had said. At that, she wondered, "What are you up to, Clara?"

When Clara took a left onto a side street, Doreen deliberately drove past, hoping she would not be seen. The street appeared to curve around, so she waited a little bit before she pulled into the left-hand turn of a mall and turned around so she was coming back and could approach the same turnoff Clara had taken from the opposite direction.

Clara's vehicle was parked in a driveway about five houses in. Several other vehicles were parked there—it looked more like a mechanic's dream shop than a residence. Vehicles without wheels were on the side; another older car had its hood open. The inside of the garage was filled with vehicles. She kept on driving but noted the address. When she got to the end of the block, she wrote down the address and texted it to Mack.

Instead of texting her back, he called and asked, "What's with the address?

"I need to know who owns the house."

"Why do you want to know?"

"Because it's important," she snapped. She parked several houses up and out of the way so she could keep an eye on Clara's car.

"Why?"

"Because Clara just showed me Crystal's bedroom in her husband's house and in her home. I found a picture of Crystal, laughing and having a grand old time with Mary, Guido, and José," she said impatiently. "Clara kind of freaked. Next thing I know, she's driven straight out to Glenmore, and she's at that address I gave you. Now you tell me that's *not* Guido's address."

"I want you to go straight home," he said, his voice tight and hard. "Do not drive past that house. Do you hear me?"

"Meaning, it is his, right?"

"Yes," he said. "I'll send a cop to drive past the house. You go home. Do not pass them again. If they have any idea you followed her," he said, "they'll come after you. These people are not to be trifled with."

"Then you better get here and get after them before they come after me," she said coolly. "I told you before. Most of these cases involve people who don't want to talk. I've just shaken something loose, whether it was intentional or not. That picture brought up all kinds of shit for Clara."

"Was she angry? Was she worried?"

"I think she was in shock. She said she didn't know who the men were. Then she suddenly recognized them."

"But, if Clara knew them, why would she be upset?"

Doreen noticed activity at the house. "Somebody's having a fight in the driveway. It's a large man. I can't really see who it is, but he's got his arm pointing at Clara, yelling at her to get the hell out."

And just like that, she watched Clara get into her vehicle, reverse onto the road, and take off. "Now she's leaving," Doreen said. "And he's not happy that she showed up in the first place."

"So maybe she thinks they're involved?"

"Maybe, or maybe they're all involved, and he's afraid she's bringing the cops down on them."

"You do like to get yourself in trouble, don't you?" Mack said with a heavy sigh. "Go straight home. Don't stop anywhere."

"I don't need to," she said cheerfully. "I already went to the bank and also picked up groceries. You can cook pork chops, can't you?"

"Of course I can cook pork chops," he said, but his voice was distracted.

"Good, then that's what you'll cook Friday night. I'm leaving now." She ended her call, turned her engine on, and, rather than drive past the house, she pulled a U-turn and headed up and around the block. It didn't lead back onto the main road but did take her several blocks down below. She retraced her steps, but it was hard to figure out exactly where she was. It took longer to get home than she had planned, but, by the time she finally pulled into her driveway, she was more than grateful to be home. Mugs was barking at the front door already. She unlocked the door and let Mugs out, taking a moment to cuddle him. "I know, Mugs. I hardly ever leave you alone anymore, do I?"

She pushed inside with the animals, all three of them talking to her one way or another as she spent a few minutes cuddling everybody before closing her front door. "You guys are something else. Who knew you would be such cuddle bums?"

When they were all calmed down, she headed to the kitchen, got out the treats, and gave everybody a few. She opened the kitchen door, propped it open, and then walked back inside to put on the teakettle, while she put up the rest of her groceries, mainly the canned goods in the pantry.

Her mind was buzzing with what she'd seen. Guido definitely had something to do with this, but Doreen didn't know what and how much—if anything—did Clara have to do with it? And why didn't Clara know anything about Guido in that photograph? Did Mary make a point of having her family meet Crystal? And maybe Clara didn't want them to?

Doreen wasn't exactly sure what was going on, but her mind wouldn't let it go. She put away the last of the groceries while the tea water boiled; then she made a cup and sat out on the deck at the small table and chair. She had a notepad beside her and her laptop in front of her. The light was dim, but she could still see some things. She jotted down the notes of what she'd seen, the house address, Clara's license plate, and she'd also grabbed the type of car and the time of day when she had arrived at Guido's house.

When her doorbell rang, she groaned, shut the laptop, and stood up, walking to the front door. When she opened it, she stared in surprise at Clara. Only it wasn't just Clara; it was a very angry, seething Clara. Doreen raised her eyebrows and asked, "What's the matter?"

"You followed me," she snapped.

"Yes, I did," Doreen said, calmly crossing her arms over her chest. She leaned against the doorway. "You went straight to Guido's house. *Guido*, who you said you didn't know and didn't recognize in the picture."

Clara's face worked into a shocked expression. "How did you know that's Guido's house?"

"It's pretty easy to tell," Doreen said, "and thanks for confirming it."

Clara's temper spiked. She glared at Doreen, her fingers clenching and unclenching.

"Why are you so angry?" Doreen asked. She eyed the woman carefully. Mugs was sniffing around her ankles, but he wasn't barking. Normally, if he didn't like somebody, he growled and barked. But, at this point, Mugs seemed to be unconcerned. Then again he'd been locked up all morning. Maybe this was his retaliation for Doreen leaving him, this failure to growl at her enemies. Mugs's reaction to Clara made no sense in many ways. But she didn't dare take her eyes off Clara. She'd seen way too many women strike out when Doreen turned her back.

And then, all of a sudden, Clara seemed to lose all the stuffing inside her, and tears welled up in her eyes. She wiped them and whispered, "I'm so exhausted. I just want this shit over with."

"And what shit is that?" Doreen asked, almost quivering as she got the words out.

"I want my daughter back."

"And yet, I wonder if you wanted your daughter when she was there with you for the first eight years of her life," she said, knowing she was being deliberately aggressive and hurtful. It wasn't that she wanted to hurt this woman, but she needed the truth. "You haven't spoken the truth since this all began. How do you expect anybody to find answers when you start with lies?"

Clara sagged against the porch railing. "I don't understand how you know that," she cried softly. "They weren't major lies."

"*Any* lie hinders the truth, Clara," Doreen said with emphasis, watching as now Goliath came out and wrapped his way through Clara's legs.

Clara didn't seem to notice.

Doreen didn't know what the animals were up to, but two of them were here now. She raised her gaze to Clara's face. "One small lie throws everybody into a different direction, and it wasn't just one small lie, was it?"

Clara shook her head. A heavy sigh came up from her chest as if a weight had been released. "No," she admitted. "It wasn't just one small lie. It was lots of them. I should probably go to the cops and change my statement."

"You should, especially if you ever want to find your daughter, dead or alive."

"How could she be alive?" Clara asked. "After all this time especially."

"I don't know," Doreen said, "because I haven't heard your current version yet. Why don't you start with that?"

Clara nodded. "I was supposed to look after her," she said. "Crystal was supposed to be at my house. She wasn't supposed to be at Eric's house. Eric and Mary were fighting, and Crystal didn't want to go over there on her scheduled days, and I was fighting with Eric to let Crystal stay with me. But Eric adored her, and he didn't want to lose that time he had with her. He was always fighting with Mary over Crystal's visits."

"So that night when she went missing, she wasn't even supposed to be in Eric's house?" Doreen asked for confirmation. She frowned because that, of course, changed everything. If she wasn't supposed to be there, then who would actually know she *was* there?

"No, she wasn't," Clara said, rubbing her face. "But my boyfriend was at my house too, and Crystal didn't like him. As far as I can tell, she snuck out during the night and went over to Eric's."

"Without you knowing?" Doreen was hard-pressed to keep the shock from her voice. She couldn't imagine an eight-year-old deliberately sneaking out of the house without her mother knowing and then sneaking into her father's house without him knowing.

"Exactly," Clara said. "Do you think I'm not racked with guilt over that? Crystal hated Tom, and I didn't listen to her. I was so desperate to feel wanted, to be needed, that I was happy to hook up with him."

"And what if he did something to Crystal that made her not want anything to do with him?" Doreen asked. "Did you ever check him out, like even online or maybe with an official background check? Did you ever look to see if he was eyeing your daughter a little too carefully, a little too closely?"

Clara shook her head. "I don't think he would have had time," she said. "Honestly, we were going at it like rabbits constantly."

"That would have been equally uncomfortable for your daughter," Doreen said in a dry tone. "And hardly appropriate conduct around a child."

"We didn't have sex when she was here." Then she stopped, shrugged, and said, "Okay, well, we might have. But we would have been in our bedroom."

Doreen just gave her a flat stare.

Clara raised her hands, palms up. "I was still reeling from the separation. I was in a very bad space."

"Which then meant that little Crystal was also in a bad space. Because not only were her parents separating and her whole world crumbling but her father had a new partner who didn't like her and you had a new partner who maybe liked her too much," Doreen said. "How am I doing so far?"

"You're doing fine, except for that bit about my boyfriend," Clara said her, tone turning stiff. "But Crystal still wouldn't have done anything to hurt me."

"She was probably in survival mode," Doreen said. "Looking at what she needed to do for herself. If she wasn't comfortable at either home, she needed to find another place to go."

"But that makes it sound like she was part of this whole plot to disappear," Clara protested. "And that's not likely."

"Why is that?"

"Because she was only eight, for God's sake," Clara cried out.

"Are you sure there weren't any family members she really enjoyed being with or who promised a different lifestyle?"

"I don't think any of the family would have taken her

into their bosom without telling the cops," Clara said. She stared at Doreen. "Surely. Particularly after she disappeared."

"But what if they felt they were helping her? What if they didn't like her family situation, and what she was telling them, whether true or not, made it sound like her home life was terrible?"

"Well, then they would have called the cops."

Doreen let that silence lengthen. "Were the cops ever called on you?" she asked gently.

Clara shut up.

Doreen nodded to herself. "So was it domestic violence between you and your husband or between you and your boyfriend?"

At this, Doreen could see Clara getting mad again.

"Right," Doreen said with a wave of her hand. "Both. It's not that the men were abusive. You were. How often did you hit your daughter?"

Clara stiffened indignantly.

"Remember all those little white lies?" Doreen asked. "Remember how you weren't going to tell them anymore? And you would clear the air?"

"I didn't say I ever abused her though," Clara protested. "You're putting words in my mouth."

"Maybe and maybe not," Doreen said. "Because all you're doing is lying, so you haven't yet spoken the truth."

"Okay, look. So I used to get mad, particularly during the divorce, and it got really ugly a few times. I might have hit her, but I didn't *really* hurt her."

"I think it's a case of *you didn't mean to*. As soon as you hit a child, they perceive that pain as punishment, and it also confuses the hell out of them," she said.

"None of that matters," Clara said.

"How do you figure that?" Doreen asked.

"Because she still couldn't have left on her own," Clara said. "Remember? She was only eight."

"Maybe not," Doreen said. "But the police have been looking for somebody who stole her away from you. I wonder if anybody was looking to see who might have helped her escape."

At that, Clara gave Doreen a haunted look and headed down the porch steps and onto the driveway. She raced to her car, backed out of the driveway, and ripped off so fast and at such a high speed that Doreen was afraid for Clara's well-being. "That went well," she said. *Not.*

Almost immediately, as she still stood here, Mack drove into the cul-de-sac, came into her driveway, and parked. He got out, looked behind in the direction the other car went, then turned back toward Doreen. She crossed her arms again and smiled at him. "Hey," she said.

"Was that Clara?"

"It so was Clara, a very upset Clara," she admitted. Instead of milling around his feet, this time Mugs and Goliath were jumping up, looking for attention from Mack.

He crouched down so Goliath could hop up on his lap and Mugs could sniff his face. "You and this menagerie," he said.

"Well, Thaddeus is on the railing here, waiting for you too," she said, chuckling.

Just then Thaddeus opened his mouth and said, "Clara was here. Clara was here."

She glared at him. "You know that I didn't lie about that. I did tell Mack she was here."

Thaddeus shot her a look and squawked, "Clara was here. Clara was here."

She glared at Mack, who was hiding a smile. "I didn't lie, did I?"

"No, you didn't," he said, chuckling. "Thank you for that." He stood now, walking toward her.

"Besides, what's the point?" she asked. "This bird will call me a liar every time."

"Liar, liar. Liar, liar. Liar, liar."

Mack gently stroked Thaddeus's chest and then his cheek. Thaddeus took advantage, hopped up onto the back of his hand and walked his way up to Mack's shoulder. There he gently rubbed his beak against Mack's cheek. Mack chuckled. "This is the first time he's ever done this."

"Good," she said. "That's what he does with the people who love him." She turned on her heels and walked inside with both Mugs and Goliath following.

Mack stepped inside, looked around, and said, "Wow, this looks different."

"Not different enough. I've been stacking stuff inside the garage. I still have stacks here to go to Wendy's, and it seems like I never quite get ahead," she muttered.

"Got time for coffee?"

She shot him a look. "You're lucky I just bought some. I was out."

"Then I am lucky," he said cheerfully.

"So did you drive past Guido's house?"

"I did," he said, "but driving past his house doesn't tell me anything."

"Can you pull the records to see if there's been any domestic violence reports for that household, or who lives there, what kind of activity occurs there? Hey, check to see if that area is zoned for both residential and commercial use."

"It's a house owned by a family," he said, frowning. "I'll

check zoning requirements."

"Family?" she asked, startled. "Guido is married?"

"His mom lives there, I believe. At least she lives there sometimes. She's Mexican, and they often come back and forth."

"But that wouldn't be on the police records, would it?" she asked, looking at him intently.

He chuckled and shook his head. "No. There were a couple complaints by the neighbors, and it was noted how many people were living there at the time that the officer came to check it out."

"Interesting," she said. "Actually fascinating, but, hey, who knows, right?"

She made coffee while he watched, and he said, "You appear to be very upset. What did Clara say?"

"She said she lied," Doreen said. "She lied to the police ten years ago."

"About what?" he asked, his voice sharp.

"Crystal wasn't supposed to be at her husband's house that night. She was supposed to be at home with Clara."

Mack slowly straightened from where he'd been leaning against the kitchen doorway. "What?"

"Exactly. And a few other incidents she lied about," Doreen said, and then she filled him in on the conversation she'd had with Clara.

"That changes a lot of things," Mack said.

"If it changes anything, it's huge. You can't build a case based on lies, but, of course, everybody lies, as I'm finding out."

"True. I want to talk to her," he said, his voice harsh. "She did say she would talk to the police and update her statement, right?"

"Yes. Unless she changes her mind."

"And she better have a damn good reason why she didn't do it back then."

"I highly suspect she was afraid of getting charged for child abuse," Doreen said. "The real question? Did Crystal leave on her own, or did she have help, or was she taken against her will?"

Mack wasn't looking very happy with any of the options. "For ten years," he said, "we've been going on one assumption."

"Which is why it's so important that we now get an updated statement from Clara," Doreen admitted. "Apparently Eric and Mary aren't in town this week, and Clara's still close enough to them that she looks after the house while they're gone."

Mack tapped his fingers on his arm as he thought about it. "Do you know when they're coming back?"

She shook her head. "No, but probably before the weekend."

"Today is Wednesday," he said quietly. "So maybe tomorrow or Friday?"

"I also don't know where they've gone. For all I know, that's another lie."

"Maybe I'll have a little visit with Clara." He backed out of the house, heading for the front door.

"What about coffee?" she asked.

"Hold on," he said. "I'll be right back." And he disappeared.

Chapter 27

Wednesday Afternoon ...

D OREEN WASN'T SURE what was going on, but now
that she was headed down that rabbit hole, she hoped
she could figure out something else. She started doing
research on Guido and José. She wanted to know what other
family members they had. The fact that they came from
Mexico and traveled back and forth set Doreen off on
another possibility, but she had no way to prove anything.
They couldn't have gotten Crystal a legal passport, so getting
her back and forth across the border wouldn't be easy. But, if
they had driven into the US, it might have been easy to
smuggle the child across the Mexican border, but bringing
her back to Canada was a bigger problem. And that was only
if she was old enough to come back. Which, at eighteen,
maybe she was looking to come back on her own, or maybe
she was looking to stay down there. Doreen frowned,
thinking about it.

She went onto social media, found Clara and the page
dedicated to Crystal and then added a cryptic message in a
comment. She just wrote **Time to come home yet?** and left
it at that. It wasn't long before she returned to the website

and saw multiple likes and somebody asking, **Is she alive?**

She didn't answer but checked who had liked the post. One had the same last name as Guido. She went to that Facebook page and took a look. They were in Mexico, which was interesting because that would presume then that somebody from that side of the family was keeping an eye on the page. But people liked things on social media without even thinking about who would find out. She couldn't do any research on that name because it just came up with multiple pages of Spanish she didn't understand.

But she sent a message, the same message as she'd posted earlier. **Time to come home yet?**

There was no answer, no answer, no answer. ... And then, when she poured her coffee and sat down, there was a spat of Spanish.

She copied and pasted it into Google Translate and read **Leave us alone. We don't know anything.**

She stared at it for a long moment before she spoke out loud. "If you don't know anything, why would you even talk to me?" She typed back **Maybe not but I do.**

She winced at that because she knew Mack would have a heyday with her for inciting this. Unfortunately it seemed so many of these unsolved cases were all about the lies which people perpetrated and the secrets they maintained. She waited for any more answers, but there weren't any, so she added **Ask Guido.**

She chuckled at that, and then she got up as she heard Mack arrive. She headed out onto the front doorstep to meet him, and he appeared more than angry. "Did you find Clara?"

He gave a stiff nod. "I'm meeting her downtown to go over her statement again. I'll have to take a rain check on coffee."

Doreen desperately wanted to go with him but knew she wasn't welcome. He got back into the vehicle as she watched. When he backed up, Mugs ran down the driveway behind him, barking. She called, "Come on, Mugs. Mack can't stay and visit now. Come on back."

But Mugs raced out into the cul-de-sac, barking and barking like a crazy dog. She ran out behind him, worried he'd get into traffic. "Mugs, come back here," she ordered. When he finally stopped, Mack was out of sight. She frowned, cuddled Mugs, and said, "I'm not sure what's wrong, buddy, but I can't have you racing down the road like that."

She picked up her phone and sent Mack a text. **I don't know what's wrong, but Mugs seems to think you're in trouble.**

Unfortunately she didn't get an answer.

Chapter 28

Wednesday Midafternoon …

DOREEN FORCED MUGS back up to the house. She couldn't understand his behavior, and it was distressing. Now she was worried about Mack too. What if Mugs understood Mack was in some kind of danger? She couldn't get the thought out of her mind as she kept pushing Mugs, who didn't want to go in the direction she wanted him to go in, back up to the front door. At the door, she found Goliath sitting at the top step and Thaddeus on the railing, staring at her. She quietly explained to both that they needed to stay together. Mugs just barked at her in complete indifference, or maybe it was an argument, saying, *Yeah? And who'll look after Mack?*

She hated that sense of impending danger. She sent Mack another text. **Let me know you're okay.**

She pushed the animals inside the house, and it was like chasing a herd of cats instead of just one as everybody refused to go in. She couldn't shut her front door because one or another of her animals were still outside. Finally she raised both hands in frustration and asked, "What's wrong with you guys?"

Just then she heard a door slam at her neighbor's. She looked over to see Richard glaring at her. She gave him a half a smile and a little wave. "Hello."

He just glared at her harder.

She shrugged. "Sorry. Am I disturbing you?"

"You're always disturbing me—all those darn trucks and all those men," he said with a heavy shake of his head. "It's near impossible to do anything with all that commotion."

She frowned. "The moving men?" She paused for a moment, but he never responded. "That should be much better now," she said. "They loaded up a lot of furniture, but they're done now."

He just rolled his eyes at her. "And the media?"

She waved at the cul-de-sac. "Look. It's clear," she said. In the back of her mind though, she was overjoyed because chances were it wouldn't last.

He had his hands in fists as he stared at her across their lawns. "It's clear now," he snapped. "But it sure as heck hasn't been clear very much since you arrived. This used to be a nice, peaceful area."

"I'm sure it'll go back to normal soon," she said in a soothing tone. "How's your wife?"

He just sniffed, walked inside, and slammed the door again.

"I guess we're still not friends," she said with a half laugh to the animals. "Another time maybe."

She motioned at Thaddeus to get up on her shoulder. He walked up her arm and said, "Thaddeus is okay. Thaddeus is okay." His tone was bleak, sad, and it gave her goose bumps to see the animals' reactions. He made an odd wailing sound.

"Thaddeus is okay," she murmured, stroking the feathers

on his back. "Mack is fine. He'll be coming back."

At that, Mugs barked.

She groaned and asked, "What am I supposed to do? Run after him?" And once that idea got in the back of her head, she couldn't let it go. "We don't know where he went," she snapped.

Except she did know. He was heading back to the police station.

"Fine," she said, when the animals just glared at her. She walked inside, grabbed her keys and purse, locked the front door, and motioned toward the car. As one, the cat, dog, and bird moved together. She opened the driver's side door, and they hopped up and moved over. Goliath insisted on taking the passenger's seat, making sure Mugs ended up in the footwell, but even he didn't seem to mind. And that worried Doreen even more.

With Thaddeus on her shoulder, she turned on the engine, backed out of the driveway, and drove out of the cul-de-sac. She also hit Dial on Mack's number, letting it ring. He never picked up.

She followed the road, thinking of the easiest and most common way he would take to the station. Soon she heard ambulances, and her heart froze. She sped up and headed toward the siren sounds.

As soon as she saw his vehicle—with the front end smashed and parked off on the side of the road—she pulled up on the sidewalk and hopped out, making sure the animals were locked inside. Waiting for a break in the traffic, she ran across to several police officers, Mack standing in the middle of them. She cried out, "Mack!"

He turned to look at her, and then his face lit up with surprise. "What are you doing here?"

She spread her arms out wide and said, "You could have answered my call. We were worried about you."

He pulled out his phone, looked down, and sighed. "My phone's not working. Probably from the accident."

She pointed at her car, and he looked over to see Mugs and Goliath, their faces plastered against the glass, and somewhere around the headrest was Thaddeus. "They went crazy after you left. You saw Mugs racing down the road behind you, didn't you? They wouldn't stop pestering me. They wouldn't leave me alone," she said. "I had to get them all in the vehicle and follow you. As far as they were concerned, you were in danger."

Chester and Arnold, who appeared to be helping Mack at the accident scene, came over after hearing that.

"Seriously?" Arnold asked, pushing his hat back off his head.

Doreen nodded. "They knew Mack was in danger. And this proves they were right." She stared at his vehicle and groaned. "What happened? Did you go too fast and wrap around a lamppost or something?"

At that, Chester had a hard time smothering his grin.

Mack snapped, "No, I wasn't going too fast, and, no, I didn't hit a lamppost. Somebody tried to run me off the road."

She stared at him and then looked at his car and wondered. She tried to school her expression into something that looked like compassion, but all that came out was, "Are you sure? Because your vehicle wasn't damaged in that way."

He sighed. "You aren't a forensic specialist," he said patiently. "And you're not a cop."

"No," she responded in a dry tone. "But even I can see the front end of the driver's side is where the damage is.

Anybody trying to run you off the road would have hit the back of your car."

"Quite true," he said, "unless they tried to overtake me on the road and then to force me off the road by coming in really tight and hitting my front end."

"But only if you were jerking toward him," she said, "so you smashed into him."

This time he fisted his hands on his hips and glared at her. "I turned to stop myself from being forced into the ditch," he said, "and, yes, my front end did clip his back end."

She was already looking around for whoever had dared to run Mack off the road. "Did you catch him?" she cried out, peering through the crowd. "Surely he's not already down at the station, is he?"

"I didn't catch him," he said. "My vehicle gave up the ghost, and he took off."

"Drat. But it was a truck, wasn't it?"

He looked at her in surprise. "What makes you think it's a truck?"

"Because the front end of your car is badly damaged. You probably caught the rear end of his truck bed, and, with a decent steel bumper, your car couldn't even begin to beat that competition."

"It was an old truck."

"Did you get the license plate?"

"Of course I did. Remember? I'm a police officer."

She just crossed her arms over her chest. "And remember? I'm the caretaker of the animal menagerie who wouldn't let me rest because they thought you were in trouble," she roared.

At that, silence enveloped the group. And then Mack

laughed.

She just glared at him, and she was so angry she didn't know what to do, so she stomped her foot.

At that, Chester and Arnold guffawed, both turning away out of politeness. But Mack had absolutely no problem. He reached out, snagged her up, and gave her a great big hug. When he set her back down again, not only was she limp from the power of his embrace but she was also very pleased, enough so that she worried it would be evident to all.

He grinned at her and said, "Thank you. Glad to hear you care."

"*I* don't care," she snapped. "Didn't you just hear me? I said the animals care."

On that note, salvaging whatever pride she had left, she spun on her heels and went to cross the road. Instantly Mack grabbed her by the shoulders and dragged her back to safety as a great big car roared past. He groaned and said, "Could you please watch where you're going?"

And just to make sure, he waited until there was a break in traffic, then he escorted her to her car and waited while she got in.

He bent down at that point and smiled at her, his hand connecting with each of the animals in tow, letting them know he was fine. "I'm okay," he said. "Go home and rest."

"And you take care of Guido," she said. "Because his truck just ran you off the road." And she gave him a fat smile and took off, leaving him standing in the road, staring after her.

Chapter 29

Wednesday Late Afternoon ...

DOREEN HAD BEEN intent on going home, but, as she turned the corner, she found herself heading in the direction of Guido's. She remembered the cross section between the streets as she had gotten back onto the main road, but she hadn't figured out how to get there directly. It took her a little bit to get onto the right road, but finally she was heading out Glenmore way and looking for something familiar as a landmark to show her where Guido's house was. The only way Guido could have come after Mack was if Clara had called him.

If Clara had called him and said Mack was asking questions and she was going to the police to tell them something, then maybe Guido would have tried to run Mack off the road.

The section of road they had been on was mostly fields, but there were ditches with some big rocks. It could have been just an impulse on Guido's part. If somebody was trying to kill Mack, there had to be an easier way, but then she thought about the ditch and realized Mack probably would have ended up rolled or flipped several times out in the field, and that could quite possibly have taken him out. Just that thought made her angry enough that, when she caught sight of the intersection and recognized the house on the corner, she did a very quick left turn and whipped across traffic just in time.

As she approached the house, a truck had been moved into the very back of the yard, and big wooden gates were being closed. She didn't know what kind of truck it was, but she caught a glimpse of gray, and then the gates shut firmly, blocking it from view. She drove past and parked where she'd been before and sent Mack a text.

Her phone rang instantly. "I told you to go home," he said in an ominous tone.

"I thought your phone was broken," she said gently.

"Well, it's working again now. Maybe it was just the shock of the accident."

"Maybe that's why I didn't go home too," she said. "At Guido's house is a truck. They just moved it into the back behind the gates on the left-hand side."

"That doesn't mean it's the truck that hit me," he said.

"Gray," she said, "I bet it was gray."

"It was," he said grudgingly, "but you stay out of this."

"As long as you send cops to check over that vehicle, I will. Otherwise, I'll take pictures of it."

At that, he cursed and swore at her. She was amazed at the breadth of his language. "Can I use some of those words too?" she asked with interest. "You know that I'm really trying to loosen up my tongue a bit."

"Every time you swear, you feel terrible," he said. "So, instead of using my words, create your own."

"So I can say fudgesicle to make up for the f-word you just used?"

At that, he groaned. "If you want to say fudgesicle as a swear word, go for it. I'd love to be there when you do."

She sniffed at that. "You should be inside a cop car, and you should be coming here right now," she said. "I'm not leaving until then. Because you know these guys will just book it out of here."

"And where do you think they'll go?" he asked.

"Back to Mexico and the rest of his family, where Crystal is," she said abruptly.

"What?" he roared. "How did you possibly figure that out?"

"It's not that hard," she said. "Really it's the most logical answer."

There was an ominous sigh on the other side of the line. "When did you figure this out?"

"This morning," she said. "I was looking for the right time to tell you my working theory, but that was harder to find than I thought."

"We will have a talk about you and that lack of sharing information …"

"We will when somebody isn't trying to kill you."

"I'm on my way toward you," he said, his voice hard. "No excuses, no more back talk, no more nothing," he said. "You lock those car doors. You stay inside your vehicle and wait until I get there."

The trouble was she had already hopped out with both the dog and the cat at her side and Thaddeus on her shoulder.

"Tell me that you'll stay locked inside the vehicle," Mack said, his tone official.

"What if I'm not in the vehicle?" she asked. "What if I'm walking on the sidewalk?"

"Oh, good Lord," she heard him say under his breath. Beside him, she could hear Chester and Arnold talking.

"What are they saying?" she demanded.

"None of your business," he said. "We will be there soon. In the meantime, you stay out of trouble and stay safe. This isn't the time to do anything heroic."

"Oh, goodness, no, of course not," she said. "I wasn't planning on doing anything heroic. But really, you know I don't like it when people hurt my friends."

On that note, she hung up on him. She laughed, and Mugs danced around. Goliath had stretched out on the hot sidewalk and just stared at her, the tip of his tail twitching. "This is a whole new area for us, guys," she said, half laughing and half wanting to dance, partly because she knew Mack was safe.

She didn't understand the psychology behind somebody who would dare take out Mack. He was a force bigger than life. And he certainly wasn't anybody to ignore or to not consider as a threat. And his attitude toward life was one she really could get behind. When her phone rang again, she looked at it and chuckled. "Hi, Nan. How are you?"

"I'm fine," she said, "but José isn't. He wanted to talk to you, but apparently you've gone and upset an apple cart."

"Is he there today?"

"He left early. He got an odd phone call and took off."

"Yeah, I'm not surprised," she said. "Does he have a gray truck, by any chance?"

"Yes, he does," Nan said. "One of those really big ones, you know? Where you almost need a ladder to get into the cab."

"Well, you and I do," Doreen said, "but guys like Mack, they can hop up with no problem."

"It's old too," Nan said.

"Was he driving it when he left?"

Nan suddenly got wind of what she was talking about. "What's happened?" she asked excitedly. "Fill me in."

"Nan, that's not really fair now, but I can give you a little insider information. Maybe you can make good use of this. I'm thinking maybe José and Guido just tried to run Mack off the road with that gray truck."

Instant silence came, and then Nan's soft gasp escaped. "Oh my," she exclaimed. "Really?"

"Yes," Doreen said. "Now you tell me. When did José leave?"

"Maybe thirty minutes ago, forty-five minutes ago, I don't know," Nan said, her voice distracted.

Doreen could hear sounds of pen markings. "What are you writing down, Nan?"

"The times," she said. "Times are very important. You know that."

"Are you placing a bet on Mack's life?" Doreen asked in an ominous tone.

"Oh, goodness, no. But now we have a race, a really good race to how long before you solve this case too, my dear. You're getting so good at this. I've got to run. Bye."

And just like that, Nan was gone too.

Chapter 30

Wednesday Late Afternoon ...

WITH BOTH NAN and Mack done with their calls, Doreen wasn't sure what she was supposed to do next. She crossed the road and walked to the corner so she could casually walk past Guido's house. Or maybe it was José's house. Maybe they both lived there. But, in her mind's eye, as far as she was concerned, this wasn't as much a child abduction as it was about finding the child. Only she was no longer a child. To get anybody else to believe it would be a different story. Mack might, but then he was caught up with the legalities of it all. It would take a little bit to get people to tell the truth.

Somehow Doreen needed Crystal to speak up. She was eighteen now. Being a Canadian, she might have had trouble getting her passport from way back when, and, if her parents never had one issued, she might have trouble getting one to come back to Canada, especially with no proof she had ever left her home country. Doreen hated to say it, but it was probably a pretty easy job to get the child smuggled into Mexico. But getting her back into Canada, her own country of birth? Well, that would have presented quite a different set of challenges. So, even if Crystal wanted to return, there would be some trouble making it happen.

If she wanted to come back to the country to stay away from her parents, that was another big one, but *this? ... This* was ready to blow wide open. She wondered if Crystal was ready for that.

Doreen walked up and down the street a couple times, letting Mugs do his business on the roadside, and waiting for Goliath, who seemed to lose interest in the purpose they were here for and instead wandered through the high grass along the sidewalk.

She saw a cop car pull into the driveway of Guido's. Mack got out and turned to look around. Arnold and Chester got out too. She was deliberately facing the sidewalk and the underbrush. No house was here; it was just an overgrown patch of city land. But she could feel his eyes boring into her back.

When she figured it was safe, she turned casually to find him standing at the front doorstep, knocking on the door, but still staring at her. She gave him a small smile and kept walking up the street. She didn't want to go too far because she knew things could get ugly fast. But no one ever answered the door. And, if Mack didn't have a search warrant, could he check the grounds? As it was, he walked over to the fence, and Mack was tall, so he could see over it.

As soon as he saw the vehicle on the other side, he pulled out his phone and made some calls. At that point the front door opened, and a woman stepped out. Doreen was too far away to hear what the woman said, but Mack and the two cops talked to her, and Doreen could see Mack pointing at the vehicle in the backyard. The woman had her hands up, as if to say she didn't know anything, but she was obviously not telling anyone anything either. From where she stood, Doreen could see somebody in the backyard. He ran for the back fence and jumped over it.

She called Mack as she watched the stranger climb the fence. When he answered, she said, "He's going over the back fence to your right."

Mack broke to the side, one cop with him, the other disappearing in the other direction. They ran to the side of the house where the person was already scaling the fence. The guy saw Mack and took off, jumping over a second fence to a different yard.

But she'd pointed Mack in the right direction. With a beam of happiness, she walked back to her car and thought about the location of the other houses, wondering if she could catch the guy. She got everybody back into her vehicle and started it up, slowly moving past Guido's house. She took a right and then another right, and, just as she was coming around the block, she almost hit a man racing across the road. As a matter of fact, he partially slammed into her fender, glared at her, punched the hood with his fist, and then kept running across the street. Mack was right on his heels, both cops now behind him.

Mack gave her a thumbs-up because, in effect, she'd slowed the guy down.

She grinned as Mack took a flying leap and tackled the guy running away. They both went down in a tumble on the sidewalk across the road. She sat here and waited. Nobody else seemed to come out of the houses; nobody else seemed to give a damn. But Mack was on his feet and had the intruder with handcuffs already on, his hands behind his back. Mack stood the man up and gave him a good shake. Doreen, not to be left out, hopped from her car. She still had

Thaddeus on her shoulder, and both Mugs and Goliath had jumped out when she had.

The guy stared at Mack resentfully. "I didn't do anything."

"No, but you ran out as soon as the police arrived at your front door," Doreen said, interfering as usual. "So you have to be up to something suspicious," she said, her voice super cheerful. "You're José, aren't you?" He would have glared at her more if he could have. As it was, figurative steam came out his ears. She nodded. "I'm sorry. I really did want to talk to you. I didn't realize you were heading out to run poor Mack here off the road. But I guess you heard I talked to Clara?"

He seemed to wilt as he heard Clara's name.

Doreen nodded. "You really do need to watch out for things like that," she said. "Clara is just bad news."

"She's terrible," José cried out. "She treated that little girl horribly."

"But then most of the women in your life are like that, aren't they?" she said gently. "Look at Mary. Mary doesn't like children."

José nodded. "She didn't want anything to do with them. She just wanted Eric for herself," he said, curling up his lip. "As if that guy is worth it."

"But maybe she wasn't worth him either," Doreen said quietly. "That little girl suffered though, didn't she?"

He nodded. "We knew the family before Mary got close to them. My brother and I used to work for Eric. We worked at his pawn shop, did various jobs. We tried to stay clean, but it's hard when you're an immigrant. We loved little Crystal. We were going through the process to get our citizenship, but we still had ties to Mexico, and Eric used to treat us badly sometimes. We'd leave, go back, and remember why we hated Mexico. Then we'd return to Canada again. It was like we needed a sabbatical," he admitted, his voice heavy. "But every time we came back, Eric was still yelling and screaming at his little girl. And that wife of his was no better."

"Clara?" she asked. "Clara was no better, you're saying?"

He nodded. "He would hit her. Clara would hit her, and always the little girl would take it. She'd be this big ghost. She was always so friendly and happy, and they made sure to hit her where it wasn't visible. But Guido and I, we couldn't stand it. We had a baby sister, and she died from abuse," he said. "Mary was older than us, and she didn't get the same beatings as the little ones. But Kasey, our little sister, she was always getting hit, and she died. We just knew little Crystal would die soon too."

"So what started it?" she asked. "Did you talk to Crystal about it?"

"She was crying one night. It was terrible. I saw both Mary and Eric hit her, and I knew her life would be even worse now that Mary was there. I don't know if Mary had anything to do with our sister's death or not," he said. "I hope not. But I can't be sure."

Mack looked from one to the other. "So you tried to rescue Crystal?" he asked.

José nodded. "She needed a life before she ended up in a box. We loved our little sister, but there wasn't anything we could do to help her. Every time we tried, we got beat too," he said. "We were all small. But something about seeing Crystal in the same situation and knowing nobody was there to help her angered us. We tried to help our sister, and we couldn't, but maybe we could help Crystal."

"Crystal is old enough to come back," Doreen said. "It might be good for her to come back and to face it."

José looked at her, fear in his eyes. "But they won't let her. We don't have papers for her."

"She was born here," Doreen said firmly. "She's a Canadian citizen. She just needs some proof so she can get her papers to cross back again."

Mack looked at her and said, "What am I missing?"

"Guido and José smuggled her out of the country back to their hometown," Doreen said. "And there she spent ten happy years away from the abuse she had lived with here," she continued, "but now she's eighteen. And her whole life is ahead of her, but, because they smuggled her out, they have no way to get her back in," she said simply.

"We tried to get her papers, but Eric wouldn't let us see any of her papers at all."

"Did Eric know what you did?"

José shook his head. "No, we had stopped in that night. I had seen Crystal in her room, crying, staring out the window, and I held up my finger to quiet her. She just nodded, but her eyes were these huge wells of pain," he said sadly. "I couldn't do anything about it. Eric was being his usual jerk self and trying to cheat us, and my sister was just laughing. After we got paid, Guido took the vehicle, drove down to the end of the block, but I snuck around the house with the ladder, crept inside, and helped Crystal out. She took a few of her favorite things with her, and then we were gone."

"And that was it? You just took her to Mexico like that?"

He nodded. "I drove her across the border. It's a long trip down south to Mexico from Canada, but I knew I could do it, and I had to. She was already crying and hurting. She kept saying she wanted to go home, but I knew she didn't really want to. As soon as I got her to my home in Mexico, I knew my mom would look after her."

"The same mom who looked after your little sister?" Mack asked in a hard tone. "You kidnapped a little girl, and you took her all the way to Mexico from here?"

"I didn't kidnap her," José said. "She wanted to go. She just got lonesome, and I knew she would be fine once my mother had her. And, yes," he said, "the same mother who lost our little Kasey. But little Kasey was beaten along with my mother," he said sadly. "My father was a bad man, and I think Mary is the same. As long as she has no children around her, maybe it's okay. I don't know. But, for little Kasey, there was no hope. We were his sons, so we were safe as we continued to grow up." He shook his head. "And I don't know why Mary was safe, but she was his favorite."

"So Crystal, she's alive and well?" Doreen wanted confirmation.

José nodded, his face brightening into a big smile. "We talk to her all the time," he said. "She's really happy."

"You know the police need to talk to her too, right?"

He nodded. "Crystal was talking about coming back to go to school. She's graduated, and now she wants to go to university," he said proudly. "We've been putting money together in a fund for her. But we didn't know how to bring her back."

"It is difficult," Doreen said quietly, "but it's not impossible." She turned to Mack to find him looking oddly at her. She gave him an encouraging smile. "I'm sure you can help, can't you?" she asked.

He just rolled his eyes and said, "I'm more than happy to take a kidnapper back to the police station," he said, "and then I'll go pick up Crystal's child-abusing parents and talk to them."

He turned to look at José. "I'm sure Eric must have suspected you. Why wouldn't he turn you in?"

"Mary," he said simply.

"Do you really think she cares about you that much?" Doreen asked.

He shook his head. "No, not at all. But we were paying her for her silence."

"Right, so money talks." Mack shook his head. "Let me get this straight. You steal his child, take her to somebody else to raise, and your sister knows about all this. Then you pay her to be quiet about it, is that it?"

"Kinda. Eric and Mary really are two of a kind. For years, he'd been blackmailing us because we didn't have our papers, and we were working for him anyway," José said. "When we got our citizenship documents, we wouldn't pay Eric anymore. But now we could tell the cops about him blackmailing us, if we wanted to. Mary, however, wanted us to go back to Mexico, so she threatened to tell the cops what we'd done with Crystal if we didn't pay her. And, once you get into a situation like this, there's just no getting out of it."

"There still isn't," Mack said, pushing José in front of him. "There'll be a hell of a lot of legal paperwork involved in this mess, and you won't get away scot-free."

"Maybe not," José said as he turned to look at Doreen, still standing on the side of the road where she'd been before Mack moved him. "But at least Crystal is safe. That's what's important."

"Did Clara know?" Doreen asked.

José's shoulders sagged. "I think she suspected. But something changed recently." He glared at Doreen. "Probably you. I was going to ask for your help in bringing Crystal home but you ruined everything."

"She's good at that," Mack said. "Where's the ladder you used?"

"Guido's house. Hooked on the inside of the fence." His voice turned sullen. It wasn't a bright future ahead of him. He'd done what he'd done for the best of reasons but…

Doreen's heart ached for him because he was right. *That* was exactly what was important. Crystal needed to be safe. And how did one deal with the consequences of this nightmare?

The cops put José in the back of their car. Doreen rounded up her menagerie and got them back into her vehicle and headed home. She couldn't imagine what the gossip mill would do with this information when they found out what had happened, but there was an awful lot the gossipers could do.

It was just bad news. All-around bad news.

But that hadn't deterred her yet.

Chapter 31

Wednesday Late Afternoon ...

BACK HOME, THE animals tumbled out of the vehicle and walked proudly up to the front door. "I don't know why you're so pleased with yourselves," Doreen scolded. "Mack is mad at us again."

Not that she would focus on that. Because, of course, another major case was breaking, and the good news was, Crystal was alive. But she frowned as she thought about that. "What about the second footprint?"

Then it hit her. She pulled out her phone and called Mack.

"I don't have time to talk to you right now," he growled.

"Maybe not, but you need to hear what I have to say," she said urgently.

"What's the matter?" he asked, his voice sharpening.

She replied, "I agree that José probably took Crystal to help her. But I think they also picked out a second girl who was in trouble, and, when they went there the first time, they couldn't get her because they were interrupted. Or maybe she was too sick to travel. They had grabbed her toys first, throwing them out the window, but then, when they couldn't get her, they took off. So only her toys went missing."

He sucked in his breath. "Right. You're thinking about the case from a few days ago."

"I suggest you make sure that little girl is not being abused," she said, "because that seems to be why these brothers are doing this. Also we need to find out if they've taken any others. I get that Crystal was probably the first, but that does not mean she was the last."

She hung up and turned around, desperately in need of that cup of comforting tea, but her mind was just buzzing. To the animals she tried to explain. "Probably because of the kind of work they did, or maybe from casing houses for break-ins, they're finding children in tough situations."

She doubted Mack had considered something like that. Who would? It wasn't a normal problem or a normal thought process. A ladder would have given them that weird footprint. And, as she thought about it, she wondered about the brothers. José ran pretty well, but what about Guido? Where was he? The questions raced through her mind as she walked into the kitchen, sat down, and wrote the loose threads on her notepad. "When they find Crystal, how many other young girls would they find? Does José have any at the house with him? Where's Guido?" And the next one she added was "What was Mary's role in this?"

She sat back as the teakettle boiled and said, "I don't get Mary's part."

Mugs woofed. And then he woofed again, and then he woofed again. Doreen looked at him in surprise. He was at the back door. She opened the door and let him out. "Not sure what you're in a rush for," she stated, but he headed down the steps at top speed. She propped open the kitchen door, letting Goliath outside too. Thaddeus waddled out, and, at the top step, he flew down to the garden bed. And just then Doreen saw a woman standing half-hidden along the corner of the house. Mugs raced toward her, Doreen silently running after Mugs.

The woman glared at him and said, "You filthy thing, get away from me."

Doreen looked up, recognized her features, and nodded. "Hello, Mary."

Mary glared at her.

"I guess you aren't out of town, are you?" Doreen asked.

Mary just shrugged. "Eric is. So I usually leave too."

"Sure, otherwise you'd have to take care of the place, wouldn't you?"

Mary tilted her head up. "You don't know anything about me," she snapped.

"I know you don't like children or pets," Doreen said. "How many other kids have you abused?"

Mary stared at her in surprise. "None, I just don't want any around me. That doesn't make me an abuser."

"And yet, your brother saw you hit Crystal."

"I only hit her a couple times," she said. "I think an awful lot of my father is in me. Which is one of the reasons why I don't want children around. I don't want to face that."

"That's probably good," Doreen said. "Better to acknowledge your weaknesses." She wondered why Mary was here. "So do you find these kids for them?"

Mary looked at her, and just a hint of fear was in her gaze. Doreen thought about it and said, "That's what they do, isn't it? Find children in trouble so they can rescue them."

"They're idiots," Mary said. "They have one success, so

it goes to their heads."

"Ah, so you did know. How many times have they tried since?"

"They don't kidnap anybody if they don't have to," she said. "Sometimes they just remove the abuser. Or they help the parent being abused and their children to escape. I think, over the last ten years, they've probably helped about one a year," she said, "but they certainly haven't taken all the kids away. The last two came out of Vernon. Both women were being beaten and the children were just starting to be beaten. My brothers paid for the women to move back east with their families," she said proudly. "There's nothing criminal or wrong about that."

"No, not at all," Doreen said. "Except that Crystal was only eight at the time, so I'm sure the courts will make them pay for it anyway."

"Maybe," Mary said, "and, if they'd left it at that, they would have been fine. But, of course, they didn't."

"Meaning?"

"There's a couple kids around town," she said, "in very bad scenarios, and my brothers have been casing those places, wondering what to do."

"You mean, how to steal the children, or how to help the family?"

"Both. That's not something you can just walk up on and change in an instant," she said with a dismissive wave of her hand. She glanced at Doreen and said, "How did you figure it out?"

Doreen was stumped. "I'm not exactly sure," she said. "It just occurred to me that, if her home life wasn't all that good, maybe Crystal wanted to leave."

"Her home life was terrible," Mary said. "I tried to get

Eric to stop hitting Crystal, but he wasn't interested. And, of course, Clara was one of the worst. I knew I couldn't be around her because I'd be just as bad," she admitted. "I never hurt Kasey unless Dad was around hurting Kasey, and then I needed to be his favorite, so I would jump in and beat her too. And I'd do the same with Eric. Much better for me and Eric if Eric doesn't have children."

"How hard it must have been for Crystal that she had three abusive parents, that she lost her family because you guys couldn't control your own abusive natures," Doreen murmured.

"She's much better off without us obviously," Mary said. She sauntered forward.

Doreen stepped back ever-so-slightly. She wasn't sure what Mary was doing here, but Doreen highly doubted it was to have a cup of tea. But who knew? "What can I do for you?" Doreen asked. "You obviously came for a reason."

"To see you, of course," Mary said. "I don't want my brothers to go to jail."

"I'm not sure that's an option," Doreen said honestly, "and there certainly isn't anything I can do to change the outcome at this point."

"Are you sure?" Mary asked. "You're the one who caused all this trouble, so, if you went up to the judge and told him that you lied or that you were misguided in your suspicions, then they would be released."

"I don't think so," Doreen said. "One of your brothers just tried to run a police officer off the road."

Mary paled and pinched her lips together. "They just need to get back to Mexico. They'll stay away. I tried to get them to stay away before, but they wouldn't."

"You were afraid they'd come back and put your cushy

life in danger, weren't you?" Doreen said shrewdly. "You don't care about them as much as you're worried about how it will affect you and your nice little life."

"Eric will go to jail," Mary said.

"And likely so will you," Doreen said. "Eric's business is highly suspicious. His abusiveness toward his daughter is also suspicious, and he used to blackmail your brothers, so that's another criminal act. But, of course, if they pay for kidnapping Crystal," Doreen said, "then you'll get caught up in the same web when they tell the cops about your role in all of this, right?"

"You don't know anything," Mary cried out.

"I know you were blackmailing your own brothers too," Doreen added with a hard smile. "It's all about the money for you, isn't it?"

Mary's fists clenched.

Mugs, who had been walking around in a wide circle, had gone toward the fence and was sitting right behind Mary. Doreen eyed the basset hound. She wasn't sure what he was up to, but something here he didn't like. Goliath, on the other hand, had just walked straight up to Mary. He sat there, staring up, as if she were a supertall tree he wanted to climb. And that wouldn't go well for anybody.

Just then Doreen's phone rang. She pulled it out, and Mary said, "Don't answer that."

It was Mack. She hit Talk anyway and held it behind her back. "That's not smart. If I don't answer the phone, people will come looking for me."

"They won't find you," Mary said. "You realize why, right?"

"Why? Because your nice, steady little world will rock if I let the cops find out what your brothers did?"

"It's not even so much that," she said.

"Of course not," Doreen said. "It's all about them not finding out what you've done."

Mary just glared at her. "You don't know anything."

"Maybe not," Doreen said cheerfully. "But you can bet other people will figure it out."

"No, they won't. If you're not here, nobody will know anything," she said.

Doreen raised both hands, as if frustrated. "Seriously, why does everybody think, if they can just make me disappear, that all their problems will disappear too? The police are already involved. So let's not be stupid here."

"I have no intention of being stupid," Mary said. "But I can't have my life destroyed. I'm not going back to Mexico."

"Back to Mexico?" Doreen stared at her in surprise. "Oh my, you're not a Canadian, are you?"

Mary shook her head. "No, I can't seem to get the paperwork approved. My brothers are both Canadian, but I'm not," she said, "and I won't be sent back to Mexico."

"There's no reason to be deported," Doreen said, "if you've never done anything wrong. I think they only do that to convicted criminals and only after they've served their time." Of course, she didn't really know that—she'd never had any experience with criminals. At least not until she came to this absolutely lovely little community Nan had convinced her to now live in. Where the den of thieves lived. "I am delighted to hear Crystal is alive and well though."

"But, of course, she wants to come home," Mary said. "And I can't have that either."

At that, Doreen stiffened. "Make sure you haven't done anything to hurt that little girl," Doreen warned. "None of us will stand for that."

Mary snorted. "She likes it there. She really is having fun and thoroughly enjoying herself. She's a straight-A student and wants to come here to study to become a veterinarian," she said as if that was such a foreign concept.

"Yeah, she wants to work and make her way in life and be a success on her own," Doreen said. "I think I'd really like her."

"What do you know? My boutique store is work," Mary said. "You're nothing but a rich man's discard."

"Ouch," Doreen said in outrage. "I resent that."

"I don't care if you resent it or not," Mary said. She looked around and said, "It's really quiet here, isn't it?"

"Not so quiet that you can shoot somebody and get away with it," Doreen said.

Mary's gaze slid toward her.

Doreen nodded. "You think I don't know why you've got your hand in your purse? Why are you just standing there, as if that's a normal position?"

"And yet, you're not bothered," Mary said, puzzled. "I don't understand."

"Well, you see, even if you do kill me," Doreen said, "I know Mack will make sure you suffer the maximum penalty of the law."

"Oh, your sweetheart police officer. Ha. I don't think he'll care for very long anyway. The fact that Guido tried to run him off the road and failed doesn't mean he won't try to run him off the road a second time and not fail."

"Maybe, but I'm not sure it was Guido. I thought it was José, but now I think it was probably you," Doreen said as she thought about it. "José was at Rosemoor, but that's only a couple minutes' walk from here. You could easily have driven there, hopped into his truck, and then gone after

Mack."

Mary shifted uneasily.

Doreen stared at her and then said, "Or you were already there talking with your brother."

Mary continued to just glare at her.

Doreen shrugged. "It doesn't matter. Mack will figure it out."

Slowly Mary pulled out the revolver and said, "It won't matter because it'll be too late. I'm not going back to Mexico!"

Just then, Goliath, seeing her gun hand slowly rise, reached up onto his back legs with his claws extended, jumped up, grabbed Mary's gun arm on either side, and hung on, digging his claws into her forearm. She screamed and shook him off. Goliath went up into the air, his claws ripping through her flesh before dropping to the ground, but he took the revolver with him. Mary screamed out loud and held her arm as blood seeped through her fingers. But the gun was loose.

Doreen reached out to kick the gun away. Mary went to grab it only to have Mugs jump behind her knees and send her flying forward, until her face planted in the grass. And, if that wasn't enough of an indignity, Thaddeus now walked up and down her back, pecking at her.

"Get them off me!"

"No, I don't think so," Doreen said. "They fight pretty dirty, and I think they like their new spot to wipe their muddy feet and to peck germs all over."

Mary screamed again and tried to roll over, but Mugs was walking half on her back and half on the ground. Every time she moved, Goliath reached out and swiped at her.

Doreen had the gun off to the side safely. She crouched

in front of Mary and said, "This really isn't a good day for you."

She could hear vehicles out in the front yard. She heard Mack yelling, "Doreen?"

"Out back," she hollered.

Mary tried to get up on her hands and knees, but Goliath swatted her on the side of the face, his claws out, and she dropped down, crying out. Mack came around the corner and stopped. Doreen stood and shrugged.

"She wanted to kill me," she said by way of explanation, pointing at the handgun. "The animals didn't like that."

He stared at both women and laughed. "Look at that, Mary. You've been bested by some of the things you hate the most," he said and continued to laugh.

"Those animals have saved my bacon so many times," Doreen said with a smile. "Obviously they're my family, and we'd do anything for family." She glanced down at Mary and said, "Right, Mary?"

But Mary was too busy sobbing into the grass to answer.

That was all right. Doreen already knew the answer. It might have taken her a while to figure it out, but she knew it now.

Epilogue

Wednesday Dinnertime… on the same day she closed her last case

I T WAS CRAZY to think how quickly this case had solved itself. And really the recipe for success in this one was simply time.

Time.

Time for others to think about what they'd done. Time for Crystal to grow up and to choose her own future. Time for others to act upon what they'd done and to continue with their evil processes. Time for the brothers to continue their good work, as far as they were concerned. And time for fear to grow within the hearts of the others.

Doreen stood on the front step, Mugs and Goliath at her side, Thaddeus on her shoulder, the cops still standing around, talking with Mary in the back seat of the cop car.

She faced Mack. "I suppose Clara was at the station to give you a statement, wasn't she?"

"She arrived hours ago," he admitted. He looked at Doreen and smiled. "You going to be okay?"

"Well, this one has a happy ending, at least," Doreen said hopefully. "You will investigate the other parents, won't you?"

His face sobered. "We definitely will. And we will bring Crystal back home again."

Doreen smiled. "I can't ask for anything better."

Just then several of the neighbors approached while several news vans pulled into the cul-de-sac. Within moments, cameras were rolling. She groaned. "I guess this will never stop, will it?"

"Not as long as you keep sticking your nose where it doesn't belong," he said cheerfully.

She glared at him. "If a child gets to come home, and several cases get closed, that's good news." Then she smiled up at him. "At least I didn't get hurt this time."

"Good thing," he growled. "You still have stitches in your head from Penny. Could you please try to stay out of trouble for a while? At least until you heal?"

Just then one of the neighbors came racing toward Mack letting her sidestep the question. "Hello, hello, police?"

Mack turned to look at him. "Yes, I'm Constable Mack Moreau. What can I do for you?"

The man held out a paper bag. "You can take this away," he said. "Just a few days ago, I was working in the garden, and I know it wasn't there before then. But I did have somebody run through my yard not long ago in the evening, just as it was getting dark," he said, the words spilling out of him so fast he was hard to understand.

Mack held up a hand. "Slow down."

"I didn't know what to think of it. I was really nervous." The neighbor appeared to be in his mid-seventies at least. The small man with a whisper of gray hair on his head crunched up his face into worry lines. "Here, here, here," he said, shoving the bag at Mack. "Take it."

Mack took the bag and looked inside. His eyebrows shot up to his hairline, and he said, "Where did you find this gun?"

"That's what I mean. That's what I mean. I was working in the gardenias, and I know it wasn't there before then. But, after that man went through my backyard, I went out to continue my work the next day, and I found it. I didn't know what to do with it. I thought maybe he would come back and get it again," the man cried out. "So I just left it there. It's just me at home, and I knew nobody else would come and take it, but then, when I went out this morning, it was still there. I don't want it. I don't want it," he said, backing up. "You take it."

"Do you have a dark-brown fence?" Doreen asked. "That runs along the river?"

He turned and looked up. "Yes, yes, that's my place. I see you sometimes walking there."

She nodded. "I love that space. It's a really nice path along the creek."

"Not anymore," he said. "Not anymore." He kept backing away. "Not when people throw guns into my backyard," he said. "This used to be a nice neighborhood." Out came his finger, and he poked it in her direction. "You're the one who keeps bringing all these nasty people here."

She stared at him in surprise. "How is that possible?" she asked. "I'm the one finding and shining the light on all these nasty people who have been living here long before I arrived."

He said, "Well then, you need to find one more. You need to find whoever put that gun in my gardenia patch. It's really not good for the soil." He shot her a hard look, and then he turned and left.

Doreen looked at Mack and said in a conversational tone, "I know who dropped it."

He spun ever-so-slowly, looked at her, and said, "What?"

She beamed up at him. "Maybe we'll have a cup of tea and talk about it on another day. I think I've given you enough work for right now." She motioned toward the chaos. "Definitely another day." And she turned, called the animals to her, and said, "Don't forget. We have a cooking lesson coming up in two days. Mind you get all your paperwork done before then so you can enjoy dinner." With a big smile she walked inside and closed the door hard.

She leaned against the inside of the door and couldn't stop smiling. Mugs jumped up on his back legs, his front paws hitting her midthigh, and he woofed at her. She reached down and petted him. Goliath, not to be outdone, stretched into the exact same position. She slid down the back of the door until both animals could get at her. Thaddeus hopped up her arm to tuck into the crook of her neck. She cuddled them all and said, "Thank you so very much for saving me again today. And for caring about Mack."

She knew the absolute joy of having all these tomorrows coming to her, even more so now that the animals had saved her life once more. "Treat time," she said.

The animals went crazy. She jumped to her feet, laughing, and said, "You deserve it today, guys. You definitely deserve it today."

As she handed out treats, she couldn't help but think about the gun in the gardenias and the suspicions she had in the back of her mind. "But that's tomorrow's case," she said, chuckling. "Definitely tomorrow's case."

She was done for today.

This concludes Book 6 of Lovely Lethal Gardens: Footprints in the Ferns.
Read about Gun in the Gardenias: Lovely Lethal Gardens, Book 7

Lovely Lethal Gardens: Gun in the Gardenias (Book #7)

A new cozy mystery series from USA Today best-selling author Dale Mayer. Follow gardener and amateur sleuth Doreen Montgomery—and her amusing and mostly lovable cat, dog, and parrot—as they catch murderers and solve crimes in lovely Kelowna, British Columbia.

Riches to rags. … Chaos to more chaos. … Fire destroys evidence. … Or at least most of it!

Flush with success from solving a decade-old kidnapping case, Doreen can't wait to find out what's next in her one-woman crusade to clean up Kelowna's cold crimes. But, before she can unearth another old case to sink her teeth into, she must tie up some loose ends from the last one.

Steve Albright, fixer for the local biker gang, has made it clear that he blames Doreen for sending his friend Penny Jordan to prison. Steve even suggests that Doreen might have set up Penny Jordan. While Doreen wouldn't do that, she's afraid that other people might believe Steve. He's a popular figure in town and has a lot of friends, many of whom Doreen doesn't want to get any closer to than she must.

At least Steve doesn't have his gun anymore, having dropped that in Doreen's neighbor's gardenia bed while she chased him from her yard. Which makes Doreen think that maybe it's safe to dig into Steve's past. Until she uncovers a connection to three arson cases from years ago and is warned off by Corporal Mack Moreau.

But Doreen's never listened to Mack before, and it has all worked out thus far, so it's not like she has to listen to him now. Right?

Book 7 is available now!

To find out more visit Dale Mayer's website.

http://smarturl.it/DNGunUniversal

Get Your Free Book Now!

Have you met Charmin Marvin?

If you're ready for a new world to explore, and love ill-mannered cats, I have a series that might be your next binge read. It's called Broken Protocols, and it's a series that takes you through time-travel, mysteries, romance... and a talking cat named Charmin Marvin.

Go here and tell me where to send it!
http://smarturl.it/ArsenicBofB

Author's Note

Thank you for reading Footprints in the Ferns: Lovely Lethal Gardens, Book 6! If you enjoyed the book, please take a moment and leave a short review.

Dear reader,

I love to hear from readers, and you can contact me at my website: www.dalemayer.com or at my Facebook author page. To be informed of new releases and special offers, sign up for my newsletter or follow me on BookBub. And if you are interested in joining Dale Mayer's Reader Group, here is the Facebook sign up page.
facebook.com/groups/402384989872660

Cheers,
Dale Mayer

About the Author

Dale Mayer is a USA Today bestselling author best known for her Psychic Visions and Family Blood Ties series. Her contemporary romances are raw and full of passion and emotion (Second Chances, SKIN), her thrillers will keep you guessing (By Death series), and her romantic comedies will keep you giggling (It's a Dog's Life and Charmin Marvin Romantic Comedy series).

She honors the stories that come to her – and some of them are crazy and break all the rules and cross multiple genres!

To go with her fiction, she also writes nonfiction in many different fields with books available on resume writing, companion gardening and the US mortgage system. She has recently published her Career Essentials Series. All her books are available in print and ebook format.

Connect with Dale Mayer Online

Dale's Website – www.dalemayer.com

Twitter – @DaleMayer

Facebook – dalemayer.com/fb

BookBub – bookbub.com/authors/dale-mayer

Also by Dale Mayer

Published Adult Books:

Hathaway House
Aaron, Book 1
Brock, Book 2
Cole, Book 3
Denton, Book 4
Elliot, Book 5
Finn, Book 6

The K9 Files
Ethan, Book 1
Pierce, Book 2
Zane, Book 3
Blaze, Book 4
Lucas, Book 5
Parker, Book 6
Carter, Book 7

Lovely Lethal Gardens
Arsenic in the Azaleas, Book 1
Bones in the Begonias, Book 2
Corpse in the Carnations, Book 3
Daggers in the Dahlias, Book 4
Evidence in the Echinacea, Book 5
Footprints in the Ferns, Book 6

Gun in the Gardenias, Book 7

Psychic Vision Series
Tuesday's Child
Hide 'n Go Seek
Maddy's Floor
Garden of Sorrow
Knock Knock…
Rare Find
Eyes to the Soul
Now You See Her
Shattered
Into the Abyss
Seeds of Malice
Eye of the Falcon
Itsy-Bitsy Spider
Unmasked
Deep Beneath
From the Ashes
Psychic Visions Books 1–3
Psychic Visions Books 4–6
Psychic Visions Books 7–9

By Death Series
Touched by Death
Haunted by Death
Chilled by Death
By Death Books 1–3

Broken Protocols – Romantic Comedy Series
Cat's Meow
Cat's Pajamas

Cat's Cradle
Cat's Claus
Broken Protocols 1-4

Broken and... Mending
Skin
Scars
Scales (of Justice)
Broken but... Mending 1-3

Glory
Genesis
Tori
Celeste
Glory Trilogy

Biker Blues
Morgan: Biker Blues, Volume 1
Cash: Biker Blues, Volume 2

SEALs of Honor
Mason: SEALs of Honor, Book 1
Hawk: SEALs of Honor, Book 2
Dane: SEALs of Honor, Book 3
Swede: SEALs of Honor, Book 4
Shadow: SEALs of Honor, Book 5
Cooper: SEALs of Honor, Book 6
Markus: SEALs of Honor, Book 7
Evan: SEALs of Honor, Book 8
Mason's Wish: SEALs of Honor, Book 9
Chase: SEALs of Honor, Book 10
Brett: SEALs of Honor, Book 11
Devlin: SEALs of Honor, Book 12

Easton: SEALs of Honor, Book 13
Ryder: SEALs of Honor, Book 14
Macklin: SEALs of Honor, Book 15
Corey: SEALs of Honor, Book 16
Warrick: SEALs of Honor, Book 17
Tanner: SEALs of Honor, Book 18
Jackson: SEALs of Honor, Book 19
Kanen: SEALs of Honor, Book 20
Nelson: SEALs of Honor, Book 21
SEALs of Honor, Books 1–3
SEALs of Honor, Books 4–6
SEALs of Honor, Books 7–10
SEALs of Honor, Books 11–13
SEALs of Honor, Books 14–16
SEALs of Honor, Books 17–19

Heroes for Hire

Levi's Legend: Heroes for Hire, Book 1
Stone's Surrender: Heroes for Hire, Book 2
Merk's Mistake: Heroes for Hire, Book 3
Rhodes's Reward: Heroes for Hire, Book 4
Flynn's Firecracker: Heroes for Hire, Book 5
Logan's Light: Heroes for Hire, Book 6
Harrison's Heart: Heroes for Hire, Book 7
Saul's Sweetheart: Heroes for Hire, Book 8
Dakota's Delight: Heroes for Hire, Book 9
Michael's Mercy (Part of Sleeper SEAL Series)
Tyson's Treasure: Heroes for Hire, Book 10
Jace's Jewel: Heroes for Hire, Book 11
Rory's Rose: Heroes for Hire, Book 12
Brandon's Bliss: Heroes for Hire, Book 13
Liam's Lily: Heroes for Hire, Book 14

SEALs of Steel

Collections

Standalone Novellas

Riana's Revenge
Second Chances

Published Young Adult Books:

Family Blood Ties Series
Vampire in Denial
Vampire in Distress
Vampire in Design
Vampire in Deceit
Vampire in Defiance
Vampire in Conflict
Vampire in Chaos
Vampire in Crisis
Vampire in Control
Vampire in Charge
Family Blood Ties Set 1–3
Family Blood Ties Set 1–5
Family Blood Ties Set 4–6
Family Blood Ties Set 7–9
Sian's Solution, A Family Blood Ties Series Prequel
    Novelette

Design series
Dangerous Designs
Deadly Designs
Darkest Designs
Design Series Trilogy

Standalone
In Cassie's Corner
Gem Stone (a Gemma Stone Mystery)

Published Non-Fiction Books:

Career Essentials

Career Essentials: The Résumé
Career Essentials: The Cover Letter
Career Essentials: The Interview
Career Essentials: 3 in 1

CPSIA information can be obtained
at www.ICGtesting.com
Printed in the USA
LVHW041627290819
629407LV00012B/613/P